PILAR RAMIREZ

AND THE CURSE OF SAN ZENON

ALSO BY JULIAN RANDALL

Pilar Ramirez and the Escape from Zafa

PILAR RAMIREZ

AND THE CURSE OF SAN ZENON

JULIAN RANDALL

Henry Holt and Company
New York

Henry Holt and Company, *Publishers since 1866*
Henry Holt® is a registered trademark of Macmillan Publishing Group, LLC
120 Broadway, New York, NY 10271 • mackids.com

Our books may be purchased in bulk for promotional, educational, or
business use. Please contact your local bookseller or the Macmillan Corporate
and Premium Sales Department at (800) 221-7945 ext. 5442 or by email at
MacmillanSpecialMarkets@macmillan.com.

Library of Congress Cataloging-in-Publication Data is available.

First edition, 2023
Book design by Aurora Parlagreco
Printed in the United States of America by Lakeside Book Company,
Harrisonburg, Virginia

ISBN 978-1-250-77412-5
1 3 5 7 9 10 8 6 4 2

ONE

I STARTLED AWAKE FROM THE DREAM.

"Ay, not this tontería again," I muttered, pulling my hoodie down farther over my curls and shifting in my window seat on the plane.

Lately, my dreams have been full of teeth. It's been nearly a year since I came back from my adventure on a magical island called Zafa, pero the island still lives on in my dreams. And my nightmares. I dream of baca dogs, demons running wild over ruined villages, while coconut-shaped Cucitos tear down anything they can get their gross, yellowing nails into. Storm clouds curl around the eerie white towers of El Cuco's prison fortress, La Blanca, like a ghostly hand. The jaws of a dog-demon snap against its chain, El Baca's howl swallowed by thunder.

1

It's not like the dreams come every night, but they're coming more often lately. I think it's just nerves though—after all, today's one of the biggest days of my life.

Pero this time was different—this time the dream took place in *my* world. A man in a Trujillo-era military outfit had sat in total silence, laying out goat bones in constellation-style shapes, etching symbols and figures into the bones. The man had continued his creepy ritual under the yellow light that hung from a chain in his room. Pues, I hadn't known who this dude was, pero ever since they'd kidnapped my cousin Natasha fifty years ago, anybody in that uniform spelled trouble—whether it's El Cuco or just some random member of Trujillo's secret police, the Servicio de Intelligencia Militar (SIM).

I had no idea what the dreams meant, but it couldn't be anything good.

I was about to try to squeeze out some more sleep, but then I felt a sharp, insistent pain in my right shoulder. I pried one of my eyes open to see what could possibly be attacking me. Pues, I should have known.

Lorena's bony little fingers were jittering into my shoulder like a hummingbird.

"Ay por favor, Lorena, what is it now?"

"Don't take that tone with me, baby sister! I'm trying to help you!"

"By severing my right arm?"

"No, genius," Lorena huffed. "For your information, the pilot just said that we'll be landing in thirty-five minutes."

"Lorena," I growled, "that's thirty-two more minutes I could have been asleep!"

"Look, you little malcriada, I put a lot of effort into making you these flash cards and the least you could do is look at them! How are you going to do work on your movie if you can't understand the language?"

She had a point, pero you can't really give Lorena an inch on these kinds of things, so I faked snores until she gave up and tossed the cards in my lap.

"Desgraciada. I can't wait until this moody teenager phase is a thing of the past!"

I tried to get my sleep rhythm back, pero it was a lost cause, and already the dream was fading from my memory. A couple of weeks ago I'd come home from school as fast as I could porque Mami said Lorena had big news and a guest on the way. Normally Mami is always good to roll out the red carpet whenever Lorena has a new girlfriend, pero this time things were different. Lorena's guest was Professor Dominguez, the professor whose office had stored the magical sheet of paper that I fell through into Zafa last summer.

Turns out, Dominguez got a massive grant from some organization, The United Hispaniola Research Fund, to take the whole family on a trip with him to DR. The pamphlet looked super legit y todo, a shimmering silver medallion at the top with a proud goat looking out from the top of a mountain. After thirteen years of never seeing the island, all the delays, all the times our plans had fallen through at the last minute, today's the day I see the Dominican Republic.

I was still a little annoyed at Lorena for interrupting me while I was trying to remember the dream, even if she'd just been trying to help in her Lorena way. Details started trickling back in. The man in the dream had been pale and sported a mustache so thin it almost looked like a trick of the light. He had moved a bone in the middle of the elaborate constellation display, causing a broad crimson line of light to flit from one bone to the other like the most depressing pinball machine ever. A smile had finally flickered across the man's face, sweat pooling in the deep creases around his mouth.

And then the light had vanished.

The man's smile had sputtered like an old car and

died. His mouth had twisted with rage. He'd slammed his hands down on the display, sending the bones flying into the air where they hung, suspended for just a moment, before exploding with red light, leaving only the outline of the man. When the dust had cleared, there stood a different man in the rags of a uniform, hands clawing at his eyes. Or where his eyes should be. Pero when he'd looked up, his face had no eyes, no nose, only a mouth ringed with tiny fangs.

Minutes later, that image still gives me the creeps.

I couldn't shake the feeling that I knew that faceless dude. Pero, on the other hand, wouldn't I remember meeting a dude with no face? All these dreams must have been making me paranoid, entiendes? I squeezed my eyes shut tight to try and remember more of the dream, but it was no use; The Mystery of Spoonface and the Explosion would have to wait. I opened the window and let the glare of sunlight hit Lorena in the eyes just in time for the captain to announce that we were beginning our descent.

I looked out the window to see the first blue spots poking through the thin stretches in the sea of clouds below us. Pues, it looked like the ocean at the edge of the beach in Zafa. I smirked a bit remembering how much seeing the bleach-white waves with blue crests had freaked me out when I'd first arrived. I'd thought that would be the worst and most confusing thing I'd see, pero it barely cracked the top five.

Then the clouds thinned, the smirk fell off my face, and my mouth formed a perfect O as I saw the Dominican Republic, Mami's island, for the very first time.

The ocean stretched out and out to what seemed like the edge of the world. I'd never seen an ocean before and now it made sense that the sky would be blue, like it was jealous of the sea. Beneath us I could see Santo Domingo, and even hundreds of feet in the air I could feel that it was everything I had dreamed and more, entiendes? The thin, winding streets sprawled out like a labyrinth, and even from our great height cars winked in the bald, yellow sunlight like sea glass.

I could have looked out at that moment forever. Pero then—

"Oye, hermanita, scoot your big ol' head to the side!" Lorena whined. "You're not the only one seeing this place for the first time!"

I responded with the peak of maturity and stuck my tongue out at her. "Shouldn't have chosen the middle seat if you wanted to see."

"You know I get carsick!"

"Pilar Violeta Ramirez, let your sister look out the window!" Mami whisper-shouted from across the aisle. "People are staring, yo me muera."

Darn, we haven't even been in the country five minutes and Mami already called me by my full name.

I bit my tongue and leaned back trying to ignore Lorena's big smirk as she leaned over me with her ~~equally~~ even bigger head.

I looked at Mami across the aisle to see if she had cooled off and was excited to be home. Pero she had a far-off look in her eyes, and her mouth cut a slash across her face as Abuela squeezed her wise, calloused fingers around Mami's own.

I tapped Lorena's shoulder. She looked annoyed until I pointed at Mami and Abuela huddled over each other, eyes closed and whispering as if they were trading prayers. Lorena frowned.

"I was afraid this might happen," Lorena muttered. "She hasn't been home in a very long time and I think she's a little freaked out is all. Last time she left here, cousin Natasha was kidnapped and . . ."

I felt my gut clench at the mention of Natasha and fought to keep my face neutral. Because I was hiding a big secret. A your-cousin-has-come-back-from-the-dead kinda secret. And an

7

I-traveled-to-a-magical-island-and-squared-off-with-demons kinda secret. Truth was, I still hadn't told my family about Natasha and Zafa. Even with the footage I had to prove it, and Natasha's video to Mami and Abuela explaining what had happened to her, I just couldn't find the right time to completely upend their lives like the news had upended mine.

"You know how Mami doesn't always . . ." Lorena tapped her chin ". . . answer questions about the old days?"

I nodded. Pues, not for nothing, but it was really like pulling teeth with Mami and Abuela to try to get them to break their silence about that time in their lives.

"It's just the way trauma is sometimes. Trujillo's been gone fifty years, pero to Mami that danger will always be a little realer and nearer than it ever could be to us, you understand?"

I did. As I watched Mami, I thought about my best friend from Zafa, Carmen, and her perfect ciguapa memory, and how it was a curse as much as a blessing to remember where you came from and everything that might be waiting for you there. Pues, Mami has always been like a superhero to me, pero it is easy to forget that before she was anything else, Mami was a daughter, and sometimes a daughter needs her mother's hand more than anything else.

The plane's wheels screamed across the tarmac and immediately the plane was filled with thunderous applause. I joined in, and a wide smile split my face. We were here! I eyed Mami and Abuela to see if they were okay, and they were both clapping as well, even if Mami's eyes were still far away. Pero we'd made it! After fifty years, Mami was finally home.

TWO

WHEN WE STEPPED OUT OF the airport to call a taxi, the heat smacked me in the face like a wall. Pues, no wonder Mami was always complaining about the winter in Chicago. I knew a little bit about heat from being on Zafa, pero this was on another level.

"¡Bienvenidos a Santo Domingo!" Professor Dominguez crowed at the top of his voice. "Ay dios santificado, there really is no place like home!"

"It was Ciudad Trujillo when we left," Abuela muttered, staring around as the leaves of palm trees swayed in the light breeze "After all these years . . ."

Abuela trailed off and I reached out to squeeze Mami's hand, pero Lorena's was already there. I hiked my backpack higher on my shoulders and patted Abuela's arm.

"There's a lot to show you, Negrita." Abuela smiled dimly at me. "If it's still there anyway."

"Much has changed." Dominguez patted his bald spot dry and smiled apologetically. "Pero it's not all for the worse. Let's call a taxi and then we'll head over to where you'll be staying."

We all piled into a bright white taxi and pulled out onto the street with the airport shrinking in the distance on our right and the long stretch of ocean glistening in the sun to our left. Pues, there wasn't a cloud in the sky, and it seemed to bring out joy in everyone we zipped past. As Lorena chatted excitedly to Professor Dominguez about the itinerary for tomorrow, I learned that we were going to be staying in Dominguez's older cousin's apartment since he was away most of the year and Mami wouldn't hear of an Airbnb. Why? Who knows, pero Mami had put her foot down about it y se fue.

Pero none of that was on my mind, porque my face was smashed up against the glass taking a long tracking shot of the island with the camera. The documentary may have been "finished," pero a director's work is never done, y también I wanted to always remember what it was like the *first time* I saw the island. It was nothing like where I lived.

Chicago, at least the one you see in postcards, is

all steel, concrete, and windows. With buildings that tower and shimmer even in the winter, Chicago is a place where, when the sun goes missing, we build our own. Pero with the sky visible for miles, Santo Domingo was built like a place where the sun never sets. Bright paint layered over dusky yellow buildings with rectangular roofs; it looked like art to me.

The traffic was super different as well. Cars were either old or brand-new and sparkling. Pero the biggest difference was how many motorcycles there were gunning it down the highway next to us in groups of three, five, sometimes more. Weaving through the traffic like schools of mismatched fish. Pues, there was even a guy riding along in the back of a pickup truck casually tossing and catching an emerald-green aguacate that was as big as Lorena's head, and that's saying something, entiendes?

I felt something building in me like the tumbao that connects me to La Negra. I wanted that moment to stretch forever. I understood a little better why Mami's rhythm never seemed all the way right in America, why she could love this place I'd never seen as fiercely as I love Chicago. There are different magics to these lands, and maybe there's nothing worse than being separated from the magic you love best.

I swiveled in my seat and grinned at everything and nothing in particular. Old salsa wheezed through the speakers of the taxi while a motorcycle rider, his girlfriend in back, bobbed in and out of lanes like a needle and thread, sewing the traffic together. I loved the flags streaming, and the sky with only one cloud, pitch black with unspent rain.

"¡Nos necesitamos preparar por la reina!" I announced, and smiled broadly at the car.

Crickets.

"¿Pilar, qué te dijo?" Mami's grin slid half off her face in confusion.

"The . . . the cloud?" I pointed, turning off the camera. "There's rain coming, no?"

Everyone in the car looked at me like I had three heads until . . .

"Oh," Abuela said. "Pilar, you mean *lluvia*. *Lluvia* means rain, 'reina' means queen."

My heart sank. We'd only been on the island for an hour tops, and I was already making rookie mistakes? Where was Zafa's auto-translate feature when you needed it?

"It's a common mistake, hermanita!" Lorena patted my knee. "But anyway, it's a gorgeous day, there are no clouds in sight!"

"But what about that one?" I jabbed at the window again, pointing at the pitch-black cloud.

Pero nobody else seemed to see it. They all just looked at me until Lorena broke the silence with a joke. I shook my head and stared out at the ocean, that one cloud curled in on itself like a knuckle. It was there, why couldn't they see it?

The cloud felt almost alive, glaring down at me like a warning.

THREE

NIGHT ARRIVES WITH THE PROMISE of teeth.

I feel the breeze tickling my skin as I lie in wait high up in a tree, the last drops of rain from the previous storm racing each other down to the floor of El Bosque. I smell the matted stink of the troops below me. They trail one another in loose formation toward the roiling smoke. Confident, their thick, wet laughter stinks up the air as they march toward the smoke to search for survivors.

There must be retribution.

I admire the silver bands adorning each of my fingers and shift to another tree as I plot my attack. These soldiers are the stuff of nightmares, but I know what I am, who I am; I will teach them that everything fears something.

Thunder booms as the canopy of leaves above my head shifts with the charging winds. The beasts are slowing now, so I begin to reach for something at my belt, my pulse keeping time with a new storm alive between the trees. The beasts halt, and some at the back glumly kick at roots and demand to know what the holdup is ahead. At the front of the column of gloomy little trolls stands a being, a man with a thick black hat shielding his face from the rain. The Cucitos nearest him are kneeling as best they can, others wearing slobbery looks of admiration. When I look at him, both the tumbao and my heart stop for a moment, as if he is a gap in the air something even the oldest of rhythms cannot explain. But I am not afraid.

I am a curse they have no name for. If they are the children of shadows, then I am what the shadows hide from. And I feel that power until the man looks up from beneath the wide brim of his hat to my exact location above him, and he has no eyes, no nose, no features where his face ought to be, just a smooth stretch of skin, like a mirror possessed by fog.

I bolted up in bed. Distant thunder sounded over the block where Prof. Dominguez's cousin's apartment stood. Who was that woman whose eyes I'd seen behind in my dream? I didn't recognize her from my time in Zafa.

Was I starting to lose it, dreaming of people I'd never met and a magical island I'd left behind? Or was danger coming?

But we'd won, we'd defeated El Cuco, imprisoned El Baca, and freed Natasha. Zafa was safe and whole for the first time in centuries. What other threat could there be?

I rubbed sleep out of my eyes and checked the phone. Pues, it was 5:45 A.M., and already I could hear Mami churning through her morning routine in the kitchen right outside my room.

I really hoped I wasn't losing it.

FOUR

THE LIGHT STORM OF THE dawn peeled back into an eighty-three-degree morning y pues, I'm not that big of a complainer, pero how was I supposed to shoot great footage of La Zona Colonial with my glasses fogged up?

My first thought when we reached La Zona Colonial was that it looked like Zafa but with more cars, well technically . . . any cars. Pero the buildings were the same, with their elaborately carved stone doorways, and the balconies above a ceremonial city hall were threaded with flowers whose dance I couldn't name. Everyone on this street looked like a cousin we had maybe met once.

It almost made me forget my nightmare from last

night, which had felt so *real*. And the dark storm cloud only I could see. Almost.

Everyone here was ours, y pues we were theirs too as we drove down Calle de las Damas. They were Black like me and amber like Professor Dominguez and the old brass of Mami's hands. There were even skinny-armed boys playing the drums for change at the edge of the park, just like back home. When we finally stepped out of the car, the gold of the sun splashed over my face, a small breeze troubled the trees around the central square, and I took a deep, satisfied breath on my street of a thousand cousins.

"Allow me to introduce you to Dr. Alejandra Vega!" Dominguez smiled. "I've never met anyone who knows more about the history of La Zona, entiendes?" Dominguez elbowed me lightly at the end of the sentence since that's kind of my catchphrase.

Dr. Alejandra Vega wore an easy smile with perfect rows of bright teeth. She had a fully shaved head and waved breathlessly at me.

"And this must be Pilar!" Vega beamed. "Dom has been telling me all about you for months. Your documentary sounds really interesting. Let's see if we can help with that today!" She clapped and started walking regally through the square, her hands the same dark shade as mine.

The next forty minutes passed with Dr. Vega telling us an incredible amount about La Zona Colonial. She'd been doing tours around there as a side hustle for years, and it showed. Sis knew everything there was to know about the fortress and Calle de las Damas. She explained it all to the point that I could picture what it looked like hundreds of years ago, with women dressed to kill strolling down the street when the country was still dominated by the Spanish. Pues me, Vega, Lorena, and Dominguez even shared the same glare when a tour bus rolled past and the speakers said something about "The great admiral Christopher Columbus." Porque we all knew that Columbus was just a genocidal fraud, weak as El Cuco in direct sunlight, entiendes?

We sampled some mamajuana from a gift shop where Dr. Vega knew the owner's niece. It tasted so sweet and thick that I triple-checked in a mirrored refrigerator magnet that it hadn't stained my teeth dark red. Theoretically, at least according to Abuela, I'm adorable—pero there's a limit.

"So, Pilar, what do you think?" Dr. Vega grinned mischievously.

It's good, pero Abuela could make a better one, I thought.

"It's amazing!" I grinned back.

I liked Dr. Vega more than I had been planning to, honestly. Most of the time, when Lorena likes an adult I assume they're going to treat me like a baby. Pero Vega was different; she talked to me like I was a filmmaker, not a tween. Pues, that was all I really wanted most of the time.

"Do you know if there's anything here in La Zona that I could use for my documentary?" I took another sample sip of mamajuana and coughed at the sweet burn. "Like Trujillo-specific things."

"Oh, absolutely. I was saving it for last porque . . . well, it's better if I explain when we get there. Es un poquito ah, heavy?"

Five minutes later, we all were walking down Calle de las Damas *again*. Mami marched forward as if the street had been named for her and no one else.

We came to a massive stone building at the end of the street, and Dr. Vega paused in the middle of a joke I couldn't understand porque it was all in Spanish. The building wasn't as tall as La Blanca, pero it definitely felt like it had the same architect as El Cuco's prison. The windows were small, perfect rectangles that glared back at me. I felt cold for the first time all day, as if wind was slithering around in my gut.

I pulled out the camera and panned along the length of the building.

"You see this?" Dr. Vega's tone was flat. She pointed at a courtyard full of giggling children and whispering couples. I nodded, the cold feeling in my gut snaking down into my toes. "Long ago, you and I would have been down there. But as slaves, not as free people. This was where they auctioned us, our ancestors. There's never much distance between history and its sins. Pero centuries later, this became Trujillo's palace. Blessedly, that diablo is long gone, and he's dead and buried not just in San Cristobal, but he has multiple graves—also in Paris and Madrid . . ."

I could see Dr. Vega's lips moving, she was saying more, pero I wasn't hearing a word. That cold, wrong feeling swirled throughout my whole body, underneath my skin, until the only warmth on me was the flask of La Negra that hung on a necklace tucked into my shirt. We were standing next to Trujillo's palace, above the space where slave auctions had happened. How could people grin and eat tourist food where I could have once been sold? Could this have been where Trujillo was sitting when he gave the order to try and snuff out Mami and Natasha and Abuela? Was this where he'd sat when he decided we didn't matter enough to leave alive?

I had a million questions, pero the sky had gone inky with clouds like it was about to open up. I felt myself fall down, the grief of the storm loud, dark, and everywhere.

FIVE

RAIN PRICKS MY FACE IN tiny, silver needles as I sprint along the branch, hot on Cielo's and Miranda's trails. El Bosque de las Tormentas has many secrets, including where the two of them are hiding.

Oye, where could they be? I stop sprinting and perch at the edge of a branch, scanning the waiting dark. A wheel of lightning bursts above, swallowing every shadow. Then I see the edge of a foot turn the corner from one branch to another. I say nothing. I am silent dive-bombing off the branch, feeling the wind pull my face back into a wolfish grin as thunder echoes in the distance.

As soon as my feet touch the ground, I see Miranda sprinting along a branch parallel to mine, racing the rain after Cielo.

"Give it up, Miranda, she's mine!" I call out.

Pues, who needs a sister when you've got a rival?

I drive my feet harder as Cielo conjures a rope of La Negra and drops between two branches.

I shoot a look at Miranda, pero her eyes are locked dead ahead, searching for where Cielo will explode up from below the branches, like she always does. Sometimes a signature move can become a weakness when your enemy knows to expect it.

Pero this time, I look to my left and notice the three of us aren't alone as I'd thought—a dog baca is stalking Cielo from below. My heart beats double-time as another chorus of thunder booms overhead. I draw a line of La Negra from the flask at my waist and coat it over my fingertips. As I track the dog baca, I leap backward over the branch, close one eye to fix my aim, and Intend a small projectile of La Negra at the baca.

Effective, and I look cool doing it too.

Or . . . maybe not so effective. It dodges and whirls around, all interest in Cielo abandoned now and focused on me. How lucky.

"Carajo!" I shout, fumbling for the cap of the flask as the baca bounds toward me, ash-gray teeth filed to needle-sharp points.

"Stay back, Cielo!" Miranda shouts, but her order goes ignored.

"Rosa!!" Cielo calls out, jumping down onto the baca's back. I hear a crack and an earsplitting howl from the devil dog.

The baca screams in frustration as it bucks and swivels, trying to throw off Cielo, her cornrows dancing in the purple light of El Bosque.

"Gotta do everything myself, I swear to La Negra!!" a voice calls from behind me.

I haven't even had a second to turn around before Miranda's there, arms craned before her, Intending a rope of La Negra around the baca's left paw as I finally get the stopper out of my flask and Intend a rope around the demon's right paw.

"Any. Time. Now. Would. Be—" Cielo yelps as the baca thrashes and barks and whines.

"Now!" Miranda calls out. Her dark oak hands tighten around the rope, pulling for dear life. A second later the baca's head splits open down the middle and explodes in a puff of ash.

"Pew, puh." Cielo coughs and spits dust and ash onto the ground.

"What were you thinking?!" Miranda punches me in the shoulder.

"Hey!" I scowl. "At least I saw the baca before it attacked!"

"And tried to kill it with what exactly—style points?" Miranda shoots back, pointing at Cielo. "She could have been killed!"

"*She* can hear you, Miranda!" Cielo pouts.

"Oh, that's good to know since you don't seem to hear me when I'm shouting basic training instructions! Acting a fool when I scream at you not to jump on a demon's back with no plan. Cool, great, glad we had this talk." Miranda rolls her eyes. "You always do this. *Think*, or one day neither of us will be able to save you."

It is deadly quiet in the clearing as the rain starts to lighten.

"It's not my fault Rosa missed the shot," Cielo whines, showing her age.

"I was *innovating* y también, I didn't miss by much!" I sputter, heat rising in my face.

Minerva cracks her neck lightly to either side. "Shall we recap all of Cielo's mistakes?

1. "Rosa missed long before you jumped on the baca, yet you still attacked.
2. "Rosa's never made that shot once in her life,

but even if by some miracle she had, you always need to be on guard.

3. "Trainer Nina told us that bruja trainees should avoid taking on an enemy alone whenever possible.

"Any of those mistakes alone would be bad enough, but all of 'em together? You were *both* clearly gunning for the failure jackpot."

I glare at Miranda, about to say something, when I see that smile twitch for barely a second at the edge of her mouth.

"Fact is, Rosa's just not as good as me. And never will be." Miranda laughs. Not meanly, but as though she's welcoming me to join in. Then I feel the laughter in my own chest, like it's contagious, y a second later it takes hold of Cielo until we're all doubled over in the clearing as the rain beats the soil around us.

Finally, Cielo manages to sit up long enough to say, "Okay, well, one day when we're all full brujas, I'll show you both! It'll be Trainer Cielo to you!"

"Oh, Trainer Nina ain't gonna like that," I snort.

"Looking forward to the generation of brujas who ride the enemy into submission, honestly." Miranda smirks.

"One day, we'll run the whole nation, though." I say, gazing up at the vast canopy of trees above.

"I wouldn't want that," Miranda muses, drawing a little circle of La Negra before her and slowly rotating it in midair. "Who wants to be the general of a losing war?"

"That's why we have to win," Cielo pipes up. "El Cuco will never take me alive, I tell you that, hermana."

"Pues, me either." Pero, already my voice sounds distant.

"I'd cut that furball down in a minute if he ever tried to go toe to toe with me." Miranda flexes her thin arms. "Let him try. I'll beat him black and blue, then shave off that musty fur to see the bruises better, claro?"

And just like that, I feel myself returning to myself, Pilar Violeta "Purp" Ramirez. But before I'm back for good, I see the three of them, the three of *us*, from above, as if I'm being pulled up and into the clouds, pero all I can hear is our laughter shaking the rain from the trees.

SIX

THE GOLD OF THE MIDDAY sun slapped me back awake in Lorena's arms. I jolted upright and looked around at the concerned faces of my family, Dr. Vega, and Professor Dominguez.

My family and friends, not some rando brujitas. What a weird dream. Who were those girls? Rosa and Cielo were total strangers to me. Miranda looked kinda familiar—but I couldn't place her with my temples throbbing so hard.

What the heck was going on in my head?!

A wave of shame rolled through me as I realized I must have passed out in front of everyone.

"Lo siento." I tried to smile weakly. "I guess I—"

"Never mind that, drink this." Abuela gingerly placed a bottle of water in my hand.

"She's just dehydrated!" Mami snapped as she shooed away some concerned folks passing by.

Another wave of heat passed through me.

"I knew that red pop would be trouble." Lorena sighed.

"Pero no, it was the—where's the storm?" I tried to push my way to my feet, but Lorena had a firm grip on my wrist and pulled me back down.

"Hermanita, you gotta take it easy. You just passed out, and heat exhaustion is no joke y tambi—"

"I know what I saw!" I wrestled my wrist out of her grip and tried to stand up. "There were storm clouds all over."

"Pilar." Abuela spoke my name so softly it was almost a groan. "Negrita, sometimes the heat plays tricks on us."

"But I—"

"Why don't we just call a car and head back, mijita?" Abuela patted my hand, her callouses scraping my knuckles lightly. "You can tell me everything once we get some water in you."

I wanted to protest, I wanted to tell them that I knew something was wrong. It wasn't just the heat; what I felt—and saw—was real.

Pero, I also remembered what Mira Paredez said,

that documentaries are about trying to align what you know with what you can prove. And I couldn't prove what I'd seen, so maybe the best thing was to just take a beat. Even if it was embarrassing to have to leave the trip to La Zona early.

Minutes later, a sleek black Jetta Uber pulled around to the curb. The woman inside wore a wide white hat and enormous sunglasses that made her look like a bug who was also trying to avoid the paparazzi. She carefully scanned our faces, but her gaze stopped on mine.

For some reason, she had an almost hungry look in her eyes.

I immediately felt Abuela's hand tense in mine, her golden-brown eyes narrowing as the car doors opened and the tall woman stepped out. She made a beeline right for me, unsmiling, before Abuela stepped in her path, jaw all steel, silver hair shining like a blade in the sun.

"Ella se cayó," the driver said, pushing forward as if she meant to usher me into the car.

Pero Abuela wasn't moving an inch.

"¿Mami? ¿Qué estás haciendo?" Mami took a step forward, brow furrowed. "We have to get Pilar into the car so she can rest."

"Not this car." Abuela's voice was so quiet, it was almost swallowed by the wind.

"Ella se cayó," the driver repeated, inching forward. Abuela stepped to the side like a bodyguard.

"Grecia, I'm going to say this in English." Abuela was rigid. "Porque I want Pilar to understand. No granddaughter of mine is getting in a Volkswagen while I'm breathing." Abuela put a palm on the driver's chest. "And I'll be breathing for a while."

The driver moved to push Abuela's palm away, pero Abuela had already shoved her back hard, causing the strange woman to fling her arms out to steady herself. I could've sworn the air around her fingers shimmered hazily. A smell like rotting orange filled my nose.

The driver scowled, and Professor Dominguez stepped between her and Abuela, hurriedly saying in Spanish that we had called the car by accident. A couple of tourists and street musicians had stopped to stare at this fiery viejita, and the driver scowled and spat on the ground before getting back in the car and driving off.

Abuela turned to me, and I saw all eighty-five years of her life settle into her shoulders as she shrank back to a normal old lady, except for the grimace.

"I'm sorry you had to see that, Negrita, but I will never lose another one of my girls to those cars."

Abuela was quiet when the door to our temporary apartment clicked open, and we both decided to lie down in our separate rooms. I drifted in and out of sleep, pero I kept getting woken up by dreams that were messy with rain and teeth. Before arriving in DR, I'd thought I would prolly dream of Zafa, one island reminding me of the other, but it was getting weird how dark all the dreams were. I didn't care what anyone said; it couldn't all be heat exhaustion—could it?

Off in the next room, Abuela's snores were calm and regular. I sat and stared at the ceiling fan as the sunlight danced down the walls. And then my bag started to rattle and glow. Y pues, not even like a small rustle; we're talking the bag hitting a full-on viral-TikTok-dance level of shake.

"What in the—" I rolled out of the bed, instantly on guard, and drew La Negra out of my necklace as I hit a defensive crouch, ready to strike.

I'd been practicing with La Negra for months, honing my skills, and whatever was about to pop off, I was ready to throw hands.

Pero, I didn't have to. Porque standing right in front of me, having appeared out of thin air, was the ciguapa who'd taught me that defensive stance, her feet pointing backward and her cocky, thousand-watt smile dazzling the room. She tossed a pair of green fingerless gloves at my feet.

"Wepa, I got the room right on the second try!" Carmen yelped, punching the air. Then her smile dimmed a bit, and she gave me a quick Zafa salute, which I mirrored. "All right, well, as you might have guessed, hermana, I could use your help with something." Carmen cracked her knuckles.

SEVEN

I LOOKED AT THE GLOVES lying in my lap and then looked back up at Carmen. The ciguapa who'd become one of my best friends last summer looked calmer, pues maybe even a little older, than the last time I saw her. Pero like, also she was over two hundred years old so, y'know, perspective. Her face was still ringed by a thick curtain of black curls, and she wore a black jacket with three gold stripes along the shoulder. I knew just by looking that it was the same shapeshifting smoke shawl that La Bruja had gifted her years ago. My heart swelled seeing Carmen for the first time in nearly a year, but all my instincts told me this couldn't be just a vacation for her.

Plus, I wanted to play it cool; I've got a reputation to keep after all.

"Nice new fit." I grinned. "You look good for an old lady who just crawled out of a backpack."

"It's called making an entrance—you should try it sometime!" Carmen stuck out her tongue and flipped her hair over one shoulder. "Also, wait. You keep the Olvida in . . . a backpack where just anyone can get to it?"

"Well, it was working out pretty well for a year until some payasa pulled up with no notice!"

"It's been a year up here, huh? Pues, we never fully know how much time passes in your world. No wonder you look taller, hermanita. It looks good on you."

Carmen crossed the room and punched me lightly on the shoulder before pulling me into a huge hug. I closed my eyes and just breathed in her scent. She smelled like guava and sea salt, same as always. I held the ciguapa at arm's length and felt my face split into a wide smile for the first time since me and Abuela got back from La Zona. Speaking of . . .

"¡Oye, Abuela!"

"Okay, that's enough with the old lady jokes—"

"No, my actual abuela is asleep in the next room! Let me go check on her to make sure your *entrance* didn't wake her and then we'll find a place to talk. Something tells me you aren't just here for souvenirs."

"De verdad, not *just* for souvenirs." Carmen grinned and sighed theatrically, but I saw a muscle in her jaw tense.

I crept to the edge of Abuela's room and pumped my fist when I saw she was still asleep. Still snoring, pues even louder than before. I shot Mami and Lorena a quick text that I was feeling better, pero Abuela was asleep, and we were probably just going to sit out dinner so we'd be rested for the remainder of the trip.

When I slid back to my room, my *other* sister was staring at an air conditioner the way my best friend Celeste used to stare at her advanced math homework.

"What is this thing?" Carmen said each word slowly as if she was afraid to wake it up.

"It helps keep the room cold." I shrugged.

"And they say your world doesn't have magic." Carmen's eyes were wide before she shook her head and followed me out onto the little balcony area of the apartment.

Outside, the wind rattled the tin roof above us, sweeping little gusts of leftover rain over the lip. Carmen's face was half in shadow, and I noticed for the first time that she had small dark rings around her eyes like she hadn't slept in days. Y también, she was bouncing her leg against the wall, a quick tapping like a hi-hat drum.

"El Baca escaped," Carmen huffed out before I even could open my mouth.

"He what?! Escaped? To where??" I gasped, my mouth hanging open in shock.

"Well," Carmen sighed, shadow veiling half her face, "I was hoping you knew. Pero he's loose, and I've turned Zafa upside down trying to find him. Fina is leading a squad while I'm gone porque you know he can rip openings into your world. And, well . . ."

A ball of dread formed in my stomach as my imagination filled in what Carmen bit back. If El Baca, El Cuco's hulking demon-dog bounty hunter, was really loose, he would be looking for revenge. And if he wasn't making a move on any of the *tons* of enemies he'd sworn vengeance on in Zafa—then I, the little human who'd shattered the cursed deal El Cuco had made with Trujillo, the one that created the demon dog, was definitely Baca Public Enemy Number One.

Carmen's voice broke through the pounding of my heart in my throat. "I was supposed to catch up with you earlier today, pero I went through the wrong portal and ended up on top of this building overlooking a plaza. And what should I see when I look over the ledge but your abuela kicking and screaming at—well, I don't know."

"She was just an Uber driver, Carmen." I clenched my jaw to keep a quiver from my voice. "Abuela has bad history with the company that makes the kind of car she drove."

Carmen's mouth thinned to a grim slash. "No, whatever your abuela was kicking and screaming at didn't smell human." She sniffed. "Something's coming for you, hermanita, just like the Galipote Sisters feared. So my orders are to bring you back to Zafa so you can be under their protection in Ciudad Minerva."

"What?!" I whisper-shouted, eyeing the door to the apartment to make sure I didn't wake Abuela. "For how long?"

Carmen shrugged, pero there was a scowl on her face. "'Until the threat is neutralized,' according to Yaydil, pero you know."

Pues, I did. The face of the ciguapas' top general flashed before my eyes, her mouth a stern slash. If Gray Locks was worried enough to bring me down to Zafa, it wasn't a sleepover . . . it was witness protection. And who knows how long it would last. Or if it would even ever *end*.

"That's just another way of saying 'forever.' I can't

go to Zafa right now. My family is here, and they'll think I was kidnapped or ran away or, or, or . . ." I felt my chest tighten as my mind spiraled, and I struggled to push air into my lungs. White spots popped in my vision, and then an even worse thought hit me. "What if he finds my family?! Carmen, what if he hurts Mami or Abuela or . . . ?"

"He won't." Carmen said it so firmly and confidently I had to stop my panic attack y todo and just stare at her. It was almost reassuring.

My heart slowed as I looked in the ciguapa's eyes. Pues, we'd been through so much, y también I wanted answers about the things I'd been seeing in my dreams.

"You're right. Because we're going to hunt him down first."

Carmen stepped forward, the automatic lights on the balcony cutting on and bathing her devilish grin in honeyed light. "You had me at 'Carmen, you're right,' but good—El Baca and I still have a score to settle after all."

EIGHT

"NOW ALL WE HAVE TO do is track that mangy fugitive. You can run point on that and—"

"Gurl, what?" I looked at Carmen like she had two heads in addition to backward feet. "I mean word, I like your confidence, pero like he could be anywhere in the world right now, right? How are we supposed to track *him*? You got a find-a-baca app you ain't tell me about?"

"Pues, you worry too much." Carmen rolled her eyes. "I mean, yes he could *technically* be anywhere, pero how likely is it that he's anywhere but here?"

Okay, points were made. The world was huge, pero también El Baca's roots were here. The demon had been created when El Cuco and Trujillo had first struck their deal for Cuco to hold Trujillo's enemies, including my cousin Natasha, prisoner for all eternity in exchange for power and resources. Not to mention El Baca was likely after *me*, and here I was. Whatever that hulking dog-demon was up to, it made sense that he'd be somewhere on the island.

Carmen saw me shifting from foot to foot and the corner of her mouth twitched.

"C'mon, hermanita. Worst-case scenario, El Baca is on a murderous rampage, bent on revenge and possibly planning the end of the world."

"Wait, he's—"

"Pero *best*-case scenario, we got the band back together for a fun adventure!" Carmen finished with a little shimmy of her shoulders like a bachatera.

"I thought being in leadership would have made you more serious," I said, trying to hide the grin that was forcing its way onto my face.

Carmen scowled and stuck out her tongue. "Leadership can look lots of ways." Carmen flipped her hair dramatically. "Don't be mad that I chose Fabulous *and* Hilarious."

I snorted loudly and shot a look at the door to make sure I hadn't woken up Abuela.

"So," Carmen chimed in with a wide smile, "we a team again? I don't really know my way around here and"—Carmen wiggled her backward-facing toes—"I think I might stand out a bit more than a spy should."

Pues, again, points were made.

"All right, pero we can't be out all night! I have a curfew and my family will be back, pero let's do it, let's find that demonic furball."

Pues, it turns out that tracking someone down in a city is actually way more difficult than it looks on TV.

Me and Carmen kept to the shadows, clinging to the sides of buildings and sniffing around for El Baca's signature stink of ash and wet dog. But that perro could have been anywhere. We moved through the streets of Santo Domingo, swallowing the thick heat of the summer with every breath. Even Carmen was sweating through her jacket, and that jacket was magic, entiendes?

"Any idea where a demon dog might be in this city?" Carmen asked. "We're on your turf now."

I bit my lip. This was my world, pero it wasn't. Between me and Carmen I was supposed to be the expert, pero I couldn't even read the signs without having to stop and translate them in my head.

I was about to say that this wasn't exactly *my* world when a noise like a massive ticked-off mosquito ripped open the quiet, and Carmen jumped into a fighting stance.

"Oye, what was that? Has that mangy mutt found us?"

"Carmen, Carmen." I waved my hand in front of her face. "It's just a motorcycle."

"A what?" Carmen's shoulders relaxed a little.

I tapped my chin, confused, porque how do you explain what a motorcycle is to someone who has never seen a bike? "It's a way people get around, like it has two wheels and they go really fast and that's how people get food delivered around here."

"Pues, why don't they just climb? It sounds so loud and weird." Carmen huffed and muttered something under her breath. Then her fists unclenched slowly.

"I don't know, it's just easier." I shrugged. "We can't all be trained ciguapa officers and—"

Pero I would never finish that sentence, porque I saw something that must have been a mirage. A hazy, white, human-shaped shadow was staring at us from the end of the street. I blinked twice at it. La Negra grew red hot in the little necklace I wore, the black sand spinning until it felt like my vision was vibrating. And then the white shadow sprinted around the corner and was gone.

NINE

"SO, I'M GUESSING THAT DOESN'T happen often up here?!" Carmen huffed. She pulled level with me as we raced after the white shadow, dipping down what felt like a million side streets, alleyways, and small construction sites.

"Not . . . exactly . . . no." I struggled to keep pace with the shadow. La Negra still vibrated against me every time the necklace bounced on my collarbone. This wasn't the tumbao that came when me and La Negra moved as one in combat—it was a fire alarm. Was La Negra . . . scared? *Could* La Negra be scared? And if she could, who—or *what*—scares something as powerful as her?

"It's getting away!" Carmen gasped, pointing out the obvious as she dashed ahead of me.

The shadow shimmered like a pearl, pulling farther and farther away, swaying slightly, sidestepping people on the street who barely blinked, like they couldn't see it. Sounds of parties and dancing people swept by us as I kept running through that ninety-something-degree heat with only my little human lungs.

"Okay," Carmen said, pointing up at the wire balconies of the building above, "maybe we change tactics?"

I put two and two together and flexed my fingers in my special ciguapa gloves.

A second later, Carmen made a basket with her fingers and hurled me skyward toward the lowest balcony.

Ay dios santificado, it hurt so bad.

I clung to the railing for dear life as the impact vibrated through my bones like the wail of a bell. My hands ached; this wasn't like swinging from the branches in Zafa. Which became a bit more obvious when I saw the scruffy-bearded tío with half a cigar hanging from his mouth listening to the radio. His mouth made a perfect O as he stared at me through a window. Pues, he had a right to be surprised.

"¡PILAR, TE VAS AL PRONTO!" Carmen hollered from the balcony across the street.

So much for subtlety and keeping to the shadows. Speaking of shadows . . .

"NOW OR NEVER, HERMANA! La Sombra is getting away, nos vamos!" Carmen yelped as she swung to the next balcony with lazy grace.

I looked back at the tío, who was reaching for his camera phone.

"Umm lo siento, I hope your team wins the game!" I waved awkwardly and pushed off for the next balcony, leaving the tío with a story I was sure none of his dominoes partners were going to believe!

I started to fall into the rhythm of the chase. The mechanics of swinging between balconies and running along rooftops in Santo Domingo started to feel as natural as it possibly could, like chasing after a cloud. Me and Carmen were gaining on whatever the haze was, and when I lost sight of it for even a second La Negra would strain and hum to the left or right like the world's most aggressive compass. Whatever we were after, La Negra wanted us to find it. Pero was this an enemy? An old friend? Both?

I desperately needed answers.

No matter what, I thought, pushing my legs to keep sprinting along the next rooftop, *that little white sombra isn't getting away.*

Finally, the shadow slowed and took another hard left to double back into a barely lit park wreathed with tall trees. Luckily, there were no people there. Less lucky? The park was at least three stories down from the rooftop I was standing on.

"Carajo, now what?" I mumbled, wiping the sweat from my face as the white shadow stopped for the first time after what felt like half an hour of the most brutal fitness exam ever. It seemed to tilt its head upward at me, like it was beckoning me down. Pues, where had this let's-just-talk-this-out energy been earlier?

Carmen, for her part, never hesitated, and leapt from her much-shorter building straight down like an Olympic diver. She landed in the branches of a tree, easy as a bird.

La Negra surged again inside the necklace, and I took a deep breath as I uncorked the top and let the black sand flow out and settle along my arm in her typical intricate pattern.

"Well, glad you're so pleased." I rolled my eyes. "I have a plan . . . but I don't think either of us is going to like it."

I'd never been so grateful that La Negra doesn't really do the full sentences thing, porque maybe she would sound like Mami or Abuela or even Lorena.

Y'know, anybody with good sense and a working knowledge of physics who would lecture me not to do what I did next. Which, pues, you probably guessed it: I took a running start, spread my arms, and jumped out into the warm and waiting dark.

TEN

PUES, SOMEDAY, IF I EVER leave all this *Save the World Before High School* tontería behind and become as good a director as Mira Paredez, someone is going to ask me all the questions I'd like to ask her, including: What was the bravest thing you ever did? Or the coolest thing you ever did? Or the most foolish thing?

And I'm not saying this was definitely the winner, pero it would *at least* medal in all three categories, entiendes?

As I dive-bombed, I thought about how hard the ground would feel on impact, and how incredibly mad Mami would be if I was completely wrong about this move. And I wished I'd rehearsed it more . . . or at all. Pero, in my defense, where would I even practice something like this?

I yanked my body back out of the dive-bomb so I was upright, still plummeting toward the ground, and Intended La Negra out ahead of me to form a black ramp, like a skateboard half-pipe. I landed with a muffled thud and slid to a stop, fists already balled up, right below the tree Carmen was perched in.

Okay, actually, if we're going human world only, it was definitely the coolest thing I'd ever done; and I also never, ever wanted to do it again.

"Nicely done!" Carmen nodded approvingly from the branch directly above me.

"Agreed," warbled La Sombra.

La Negra flared along my arms, hovering in intricate patterns around my fists. My heart hammered against my chest as I glared at La Sombra.

"Okay, cardio's over. Answers, now. Who are you?"

"Wrong question," La Sombra responded, its voice shivering.

"I think we get to decide that!" Carmen spat back through clenched teeth.

"Right to business, I like that," La Sombra said. "Well, my name is none of your concern, pero un momento."

La Sombra quivered and shook like superheated air spilling out of the front seat of Mami's van. The

56

shadow melted into the air and in its place appeared a woman, her skin half glowing like a dirty pearl. Pues, her feet were pointing forward like a human's, so she wasn't a ciguapa.

Pero she didn't look all the way human either.

I couldn't put my finger on it. The strange woman seemed stretched out, unnaturally thin in places along her arms and legs. La Negra was humming so hard against my arms I couldn't tell which shook more, me or the black sand.

"That's better, right?" The pearl-skinned woman flashed what was probably once a winning smile, pero homegirl needed a dentist something fierce, entiendes? Her teeth weren't dirty, but they were almost translucent in the moonlight like a fogged-up pair of glasses.

"Not really," Carmen growled from above. "What are you, a witch? Some kind of demon?"

"Again, wrong question," the woman replied, pero her eyes were on me, unblinking. She had a hungry look, like she'd been waiting a long time to see me.

"Okay, I'll bite." I shrugged, trying to seem casual. "What is the right question?"

The woman half smiled, and her grin vaguely reminded me of someone, pero I couldn't think straight with my pulse thumping in my ears.

"My terms. For your surrender." The woman sounded almost bored, pero she didn't blink.

"Surrender to who?!" I shouted, whipping a long braid of La Negra into the ground so dust rained up into the air.

The woman took a slithering step forward, letting loose a mirthless laugh. "I had forgotten the arrogance of your kind, little bruja."

"Surrender to *who*," I growled, not backing down.

I chanced a quick look up to see if Carmen had a good fighting position in case something went down.

"The Sweatless One approaches. Soon the seas mock the skies," the woman crooned, almost like a lullaby. "Soon the howl that shook the world se regresa a la isla. The tide is already churning around you, little bruja. Soon the storm, then the world, everything will be as it was." The woman blinked her large green eyes as she gestured around at the sleeping city. "What was agreed to must be maintained. The world you love is already a memory, Pilar. The right question is: Do you want to live to see the next one?"

My jaw tensed at the mention of my name—how did this woman know who I was? Pues, there's a time for diplomacy and a time to just start punching stuff. Enough riddles.

Carmen leapt from her position in the tree, fists cocked back as she dive-bombed toward the woman.

She simply glanced upward and caught Carmen across the chin with a left hook that sent her sprawling through the dust at the edge of the park. If there was any doubt before, this woman didn't come to play. Pero neither did I.

I Intended La Negra into a circle around me and sculpted the black sand into eight separate tentacles poised to strike, just like La Bruja had done right before El Cuco breached the barrier to her secret hideout. I'd been practicing that move on my own all year and it wasn't quite as good as La Bruja's, pero she'd had a few centuries–long head start, so sue me if my eighth tentacle was kinda thin and wimpy.

The woman cocked an eyebrow at me. "Well, well, well, look who's still alive," she crooned again, looking just above me like she was talking to someone else. "You're too late, old friend."

I didn't have time to ask who she was talking to, porque she raised her arms like a puppeteer, and I was *not* down to find out what was waiting on the other end of that. Y también, Carmen was still working her way back to her feet. I shot a whip of La Negra out at the woman as hard as I could.

She caught it.

Not with her hands, pero with some invisible vise-like grip she must've conjured in the air in front of her. I felt a sickening pang ripple under my skin as I saw the rope of black sand twisting and turning like a snake suspended soundlessly above the ground. My stomach turned as individual grains of La Negra trickled to the earth, bleached and dead as the grains that had opened the locked doors of La Blanca during last year's invasion of El Cuco's now-demolished prison.

"How is tha—" I mouthed.

"You've got skill, little bruja," the woman said, fighting to keep her stretched face calm. "But a child's weapon"—she stretched her hands, sending a wave of shimmering air charging forward and knocking me off my feet—"receives a child's result."

And that was the last thing I heard before her attack washed over me, still hanging in the air as all the sound rushed out of the world.

ELEVEN

THE NEXT THING I SEE is daylight trickling through the leaves of the trees. Pues, actually, it isn't daylight; the light is a thin violet. My head is ringing like I've just gone eight rounds with Mike Tyson.

How long have I been I out?

I try to sit up, pero I can't move a muscle. I still can feel the breeze on my skin and even a couple of dewdrops from the massive circle of trees above.

Wait, dewdrops? A circle of trees? Where am I?

"ROSA! Oye, payasa, you planning on staring at the trees all day?" I hear someone call out and feel my head jerk toward the noise. I rise to rest on my elbows in the pillowy grass.

"Ugh, lucky shot," I hear a voice nearby say, before realizing it is coming from my mouth. *What is going*

61

on? Is this another dream? Why can I hear my thoughts too?!

Wait, I know that laugh, is that—

"Well, hotshot, I'd be happy to do it again, pero I won't fight a rival on the ground." The speaker, a short woman, chuckles. She is older than she was in the last dream, and her locks are much shorter and her face *way* less wrinkled than I am used to. She stretches out a hand to help me up.

"How honorable." I hear the sarcastic voice come out of my mouth as Rosa, the woman I am in this loco dream. Rosa ignores the hand, pushing our knuckles into the lush grass and forcing us to our feet. "You'll be a leader yet, if you ever learn to stop cheating, Miranda."

Miranda rolls her eyes and shrugs in a familiar way, pero it can't be. She *couldn't* be who I think she is. "Pues, La Negra calls for many leaders. Pero she also calls for patience, Rosa. You keep losing our sparring matches porque—"

"You're not Trainer Nina, I don't need your lectures," Rosa says, holding up our hand.

Miranda scowls and the expression is unmistakable, even though La Bruja looks about 450 years younger than when I'd last seen her. Pues, there she is, my mentor, the last bruja on Zafa. You can take the graying hair and wrinkles out of the bruja, pero that side-eye is one of a kind.

"All right, don't listen. The bruises I left on you speak for me, anyway." The younger La Bruja smirks.

I feel a wave of heat dance over Rosa's face and snap back to . . . well, is this reality? A dream?

Pues, have I finally gotten hit so hard I got knocked into last century? I really hope not. Lorena's the one who loves time travel movies. I barely passed pre-algebra this year—if I have to do calculus in order to escape the past, I'm pretty much doomed, entiendes?

Rosa blinks our eyes and sinks into a fighting stance.

"Again," she growls at La Bruja, anger turning her arm muscles to stone beneath her pale gold skin.

"Fine." La Bruja's eyes harden as the sounds of other sparring sessions ring in the clearing. "One more win will make it four out of six matches for me then."

Pero before anything can pop off between La Bruja and the strange girl I am stuck inside of, there is a thunderous crack behind Rosa. A second later, a massive branch collapses from the tree above, sending dust in every direction as the entire training area grinds to a halt.

"YA," booms a voice from the middle of the

clearing. "EVERYONE STOP WHAT YOU'RE DOING."

"Now look what you did," La Bruja grumbles, shooting Rosa another trademark side-eye.

"I didn't do anyth—" Rosa starts, pero a calloused hand settles on her shoulder before she can finish.

"Brujas, what is our mantra?" says a woman who just has to be Trainer Nina.

"We are the defenders of memory," Rosa says confidently.

"And the *prodigy* is already mistaken." Trainer Nina sighs. "Can anyone help out Rosa, who was apparently advanced enough to get selected recently for a ciguapa reconnaissance mission but too thick-headed to remember our credo?"

La Bruja steps in. "We are partners, and we are one. La Negra serves me no more than I serve La Negra. We are the defenders of memory, keepers of Zafa."

"Thank you, Miranda, for that admirable display of memory"—Trainer Nina pinches the bridge of her nose, and La Bruja smiles in spite of herself—"and less than admirable display of speaking out of turn," Trainer Nina finishes as La Bruja's smile evaporates.

So that's who La Bruja gets her "sense of humor" from.

"I just wanted to—"

"Cover up another mistake caused by Rosa's arrogance?" Trainer Nina arches an eyebrow.

"I wasn't being arrogant on that mission! I had the situation under control." Rosa clenches our jaw until I think our teeth might break.

"Until you didn't, right?" Trainer Nina eyes the thick log that has crashed down.

"If La Negra had only—" Rosa grunts.

"Ah, there it is! In record time no less, wepa!" Trainer Nina rolls her eyes to giggles and whispers from the surrounding brujas in training. "Once again, Rosa expects La Negra to simply bend to her will."

A wave of heat flushes Rosa's face.

"Pues, doesn't everyone make a mistake once in a while?" asks a younger bruja with a mane of brown hair pulled into a tight ponytail.

"Not in the field. Charging out into the open before the signal nearly exposed the entire group's position to the enemy. Everyone makes mistakes? Desgraciada, you didn't make a mistake; you made a choice," Trainer Nina says gravely. "And it blew up in your face, y también you don't seem to see the root of the problem. Or would you so easily lose your temper face-to-face with El Baca? With the enemy himself, El Cuco?"

"It was only a tree," grumbles Rosa, her voice shrinking.

"And why should the tree pay the price for your vanity, mija?" Trainer Nina shoots back.

Quiet rules the clearing then. Rosa's—my—fists clench, and I felt the tumbao ripple along our skin as if she is about to Intend La Negra into a weapon against Trainer Nina. But then, for the second time that day, a thunderous crack rings through the clearing. This time, nothing is broken. An older-looking bruja walks out from the trunk of a hollowed-out tree, panic in every line of her face.

"Defense positions, now!"

No further instructions are needed. Grains of La Negra swirl around every available arm as the brujas sweep up the trees. Rosa sprints to her position, neck and neck with the bruja scout who sounded the alarm.

"What's coming, Yahaira?" She gasps between long strides. "El Baca? Cucitos?"

Yahaira shakes her head and looks at Rosa, fighting the tremble in her voice. "The Pariguayo is coming."

TWELVE

STARS DANCED IN THE STILL-DARK sky as my eyes flew open. It was nighttime back in Santo Domingo, and Carmen was shaking me desperately and calling my name. Which wasn't helping my throbbing headache at all.

"Ugh, what happened?" I moaned, forcing myself up on my elbows. Carmen sported a nasty bruise on her chin.

"Well, I got punched in the face." Carmen traced the edges of the violet bruise. "And you got hit in the face by . . . well, I don't know what it was, pero we both got hit in the face."

"And she got away?" I asked.

"Pues, more like *ran* away!" Carmen scowled. "I had just recognized her smell también—she cloaks it well pero that was definitely the same sketchy lady who tried to pick you up in one of those . . . um . . ." Carmen made an engine noise and rumbled her hand along.

"Cars?" I finished for her, head still ringing. She must've been referring to the Volkswagen with that strange Uber driver that Abuela had nearly thrown hands with.

"Yeah, a . . . car. So anyway, I saw her standing over you and it was like she couldn't see anything else so—"

"Carmen." I put a hand on her shoulder. "Nena, I love you, pero we don't have time to do blow by blow. Did she say or do anything that raised a red flag besides knock us out in the first round?"

"Whatever she was, she definitely wasn't in the mood for attention from anyone but you. One second she was there, the next she dissolved into vapor when people started hearing all the tontería and coming this way. I carried you away before people could show up and start asking questions of the girl with the backward feet." Carmen's brow furrowed as she pulled me upright. "I don't know why she ran. Guess the sombra can't do that shadow trick forever and also make a quick exit? I don't know, maybe she's just a coward. I leave that kind of magic math to y'all brujas."

Great, so now we had *two* magical fugitives looking for revenge and possibly loose in my world. Plus, that white sombra had spoken in riddles; what was that all about? Pues, normally I have a great memory— nothing on Carmen's perfect photographic memory, pero I learned every lyric to Cardi B's first album in one try! But my head was throbbing, so the riddle kept coming out really chopped and screwed.

"She said something like . . . there was a 'storm,' and a 'howl.'" I massaged my temples, trying to remember the words. "Was that the same storm I've been seeing since we arrived on the island? And she said something about 'the Sweatless One.' But that doesn't make any sense. Who doesn't sweat in ninety-degree heat? Nothing human . . ."

"Pilar?" Carmen looked worriedly at me "Hermanita, are you concussed?"

"Wait . . ." The fog of my ringing head started to clear. My eyes widened with a new, terrible thought. "You said that La Sombra tried to take me at La Plaza?"

"Yes, that—"

"So she knows what my family looks like? And where to look for them?"

Carmen's eyes widened as the dots connected for her.

"We *need* to get out of here and back to where I'm staying. I saw something, a vision maybe, while I was knocked out, y yo no se. We need answers . . . and I need to make sure my family is safe. My abuela's asleep, she could—we have to go back. Now."

We took the quick way along the rooftops, the moon swelling our shadows. As we sprinted, I told Carmen about my vision y también the storm I saw en la Plaza Nacional. The whole time my pulse was jackhammering as I wondered what that strange white shadow lady might be doing to my family if I was too late. It helped to have Carmen back at my side, someone who would take me at my word no matter how wild my stories were. Pues, that's love too, entiendes?

"Well, those are definitely not coincidences." Carmen grimaced as she landed beside me in the abandoned lot next to Dominguez's cousin's apartment. "El Baca escapes, you start seeing storm clouds, and a shadow lady comes through to drop some weird messages while using a power I've never seen before and leaves both of us alive? Plus, what's a pariguayo?! Something big is going down. Pero family first. You want to go in together or should I stay out here for backup?"

I stared at the apartment, beads of sweat trailing

down my back in intricate patterns. La Negra swirled in the necklace, like someone deeply asleep having a terrible dream. I flexed my fingers and adjusted my gloves.

"Y'know, I think I'll take lead on this." I coughed to cover up the quiver in my voice. "Porque what if they're . . . I'll just take lead and whistle if I need backup."

Carmen nodded and made her hands into a little basket.

"Don't launch me so high this time." I forced a smile onto my face to look brave, but I let it slide away. If anyone knew what it was like to not know if your family was alive or dead, it was her. Plus, sisters don't need to lie to each other. We know grief has never made us weak, entiendes?

My landing on the little patio was much smoother than earlier. I slid effortlessly through the door, my heart finna pound out my chest.

At first I heard nothing. The silence stretched, and I steadied my hands as I opened the door to the hallway, afraid of what I would find. I readied La Negra, like unsheathing a machete.

Relief flooded my chest at the sound of Abuela's peaceful snores echoing around the little apartment. At least she was safe, pues, I don't know what I would've done if anything had happened to her.

That still left a bunch of questions though, like: Where was the rest of my family? Who was that evil-looking shadow lady? What did she really want, and why did she know my name? Did she know where to find Mami and Lorena?

She and El Baca could be anywhere, and even though I had no idea what evil they were planning, I had a sinking feeling they were planning it *together*, and that my family was right in the crosshairs with only me to protect them. But if I went searching for my family, I'd be leaving Abuela unprotected. I needed everything to slow down. Pues, and who knew how many allies El Baca and La Sombra had? I needed more backup, I needed my friends, I needed more time.

Time, I thought. *Claro, that might be the key after all!*

I hustled back out to the porch area and gave the all-clear signal to Carmen, who leapt up immediately.

"Okay, let's go with your original idea—we need to get back to Zafa." I unzipped my backpack and pulled out the Olvida paper. "We need to ask the Galipote

Sisters what the Pariguayo is. I just feel like we're *this* close to solving what is going on here, and that's the key."

"What about your family? That sombra lady could be coming after them."

I felt my throat tighten. "Ya, but we don't have any idea who she is or how to defeat her. Pero time runs differently in Zafa; last summer, I was with you for a week and in my world only a few hours had passed. We can try and stop the clock up here while we get some answers back in Zafa."

Carmen tapped her chin and then immediately winced when her finger hit too close to the bruise. "I—" Carmen started.

Pero she never finished that thought, porque we heard a lock clunk into place. Mami and Lorena called out my name quietly from the other side of the door to see if I was awake and could help bring in their bags. I was so relieved to hear their voices, pero I still put my arms through the straps of my bag, felt for the weight of my camera, and stuck my hand out to Carmen.

"You in, hermana?" I asked, my voice barely louder than a whisper.

The handle on the door to my room began to

jiggle, and an anxious look shook behind Carmen's eyes as she nodded wordlessly. We both slammed our hands down on the Olvida and were surrounded by piercing white light. The door to my room creaked open as I fell once again into another world.

THIRTEEN

"Y'KNOW, JUST ONCE I WOULD like to do some inter-dimensional travel that doesn't end with me getting sand in my mouth. Just once," I grumbled, spitting out what felt like half a beach.

"Pues, cost of doing business." Carmen shook her long mane of curls, sending white sand flying everywhere.

Everything in Zafa looked almost the same as when I'd left it a year ago. The ocean was still a bright white, the waves cresting blue as they roared into the shoreline. Behind me I could hear the distant thunder of El Bosque de las Tormentas. It smelled like sea salt and a bit of lavender. It smelled like home—not Chicago, but I'd forgotten home smells like this too.

Pero the real surprise came when I felt the tumbao

of La Negra under the surface of the white sand. I turned the grains over in my hands as I noticed some black flecks mixed in. Last time I'd been in Zafa, the black sand had been cut off from this beach by the evil of El Cuco and his prison, La Blanca.

"La Negra is healing Zafa still," Carmen chimed in as she stretched her shoulder. "It's going to take years, pues, generations probably, for everything to be back kinda like it was."

I felt a pang of sadness knowing there'd be whole generations of kids and adults who would never get to see Zafa healed and free of the last remnants of El Cuco's influence. Nobody should have to wait to be free, least of all the island herself, entiendes?

"But"—Carmen smiled, turning over a mostly black handful of sand—"she's healing as fast as she can. Y pues, many of us didn't expect to live to see things ever get this good again."

I smiled a bit as we started walking into El Bosque, but my smile had an edge.

Lorena went through a phase in freshman year of college when she was thinking of becoming a psychiatrist. "Every trauma," Lorena had once said, "imprints in our minds, leaving a painful memory of that moment when something unimaginable happened." She talked about how it can change everything for the brain, and I remember feeling anxious because it sounded like how Mami felt after Natasha was kidnapped. It was really scary thinking one day something could happen to me and I might just never be the same—or maybe I had already experienced my own trauma and *would* never be the same.

I looked at the purple light filtering through the trees in El Bosque, dancing in Carmen's curls, and I felt better, though. Porque she'd made a good point back on the beach. When I'd last been in El Bosque, I was running from life-threatening danger, the forest swarming with bacas and Cucitos. Pues, generations of Zafa's people and creatures had never thought they'd be able to walk through El Bosque without being kidnapped or worse. Never thought they'd see La Negra bring the island back to life.

If Lorena was right and trauma is the mind responding to something previously unimaginable, maybe freedom was reaching toward something you were told never to imagine. Maybe love is as simple as trying to make an unsafe world safe for the people you cherish.

"How far out from Ciudad Minerva do you think we are?" I asked, dipping low to avoid a spiderweb.

"A couple of hours, unless—" Carmen looked away quickly.

"Unless what?"

"Nope, forget I said anything," Carmen said, all fake casual. "We are above ground, and a couple of hours away from Minerva and the Galipote Sisters."

"Ohhh, you just don't want to take the tunnels!" I laughed.

"No," Carmen said sarcastically, flicking a wrist. "I love going extremely fast in a pitch-black tunnel with no means of escape to the outside world! Who wouldn't want to sign up for that . . . experience?"

"Carmen." I rolled my eyes.

"Fine, fine. Family first." She took a deep breath. "Do the thing where you open up the ground and I hold my breath for a bajillion years until we're back in the open air."

I nodded appreciatively and put my palms to the soil, dragging my fingers over the gnarled roots of the trees until I felt something. The tumbao of La Negra felt stronger than ever, and I was about to surrender to that rhythm I knew almost as well as I knew my own name.

Pero that eyeless face from my dream on the plane flashed before my eyes, its bleached skin and graying mouth staring right at me, and I leapt back like I'd been burned.

"Hermana." Carmen caught me in her muscular arms and immediately shifted to stand in front of me. "Did you hit your head again or something?" She cocked an eyebrow.

"No, but I think we just got some answers." I took a deep breath and put my hands to the dirt again, searching for the tumbao. "While traveling to DR, I dreamed of this eyeless face. I thought it was just a nightmare—"

"Pilar, you're not making any sense—"

"I know," I said, pinching my eyes shut as I continued searching the ground. "Pero I need you to trust me."

Carmen put a warm hand on my shoulder.

And that's when I felt the tumbao catch, and I surrendered to that feeling of connection to all of memory, the way the earth can sound just like home.

"I know where I've seen that face before," I said as I raised my arms and pulled the ground apart like a door.

FOURTEEN

IT WAS NICE TO SEE the city of Minerva recovering well from all the damage El Cuco's forces had inflicted. When I'd gone back to my world, the city had been mostly rubble and cracked windows. The Cucitos had torn down every flag, the wrought iron balconies where black roses had spun and danced in the wind were broken and splayed at weird angles. Now the city was rebuilding—slowly, pero rebuilding. Pues, some of the building that had been laid to dust were even taller than I remembered. I stared around while me and Carmen walked into the city's heart.

Y también, the people of Zafa looked so much happier than they had last time. I guess getting rid of a dictator has that effect. People played music out of open windows and the strings of a guitar in the apartment I was passing under whined something that felt spookily close to my favorite bachata song. I opened my mouth, and my jaw gave a huge pop that even shocked Carmen.

"Pues, hermanita, how hard did that blast hit you?"

"That sombra will get it twice as hard next time we see her," I answered as I rubbed my chin. "Anyway, why are people staring at us?"

Carmen blinked like I'd told her that I was going to be taking all of my allowance in the form of pastelillos. "Porque you're their hero? Did you think they'd just forget the little bruja who saved the island?"

I guess it hadn't occurred to me that people would recognize me, but the more smiling faces we passed on our way toward the looming hall of the Galipote Sisters, the more the reality sank in. Pero that didn't make it not weird, entiendes? I felt this heavy sense of pressure seeing little kids giggling and pushing one another toward me, daring their friends to come and say hello. Pues, I'm a director, so it's my job to weave events into a story; I'm not used to *being* the story.

It felt strange that there were adults, full-grown people with kids of their own, who thought of me as a hero.

"Pilar," Carmen started warmly, "I wanted to say—"

Pero Carmen cut herself off because we'd finally arrived at the Hall of the Galipotes. After the raid on La Blanca, I wasn't sure if the building at the heart of the resistance to El Cuco and home of the four Sisters whose magic kept the city safe would ever take my breath away again. But it was even more magnificent than I remembered, and I stopped walking for a moment just to admire what the people of Zafa had done.

The building had been reconstructed all in black marble with a set of massive silver doors carved with intricate patterns that told the story of Zafa, of the Galipotes, of the Resistance. And of *me*. Porque right in the middle of the new silver doors was a carving so perfect it seemed like a photograph. Me and Carmen back-to-back, fists raised against the surrounding dark, four butterflies blazing above us. I felt tears prick the backs of my eyes.

"I wanted to say," Carmen repeated softly, "that you're not alone. It might be corny to say, but whatever El Baca and that shadow lady are planning, I won't let them take your family. Te prometo."

I looked at the Pilar carved into the door; she

looked like me, pero on the cover of a movie poster. Jaw set tight, grains of La Negra navigating through the grooves that made up the carving so it almost felt like she was alive. As alive as me. This Pilar carved in the door was me too, someone I'd been.

But could I be her again when my family and my world needed me most? I thought worriedly.

I hiked my backpack up on my shoulder and stuck my hands in my pockets. I found a crumpled RD$200 note in one of my pockets and unraveled it. On it were the faces of three of the Mirabal Sisters, the fearless women who had stood up to Trujillo and his evil henchmen, shining like saints on bodega candles. All of their jaws were set like the versions of Carmen and me carved into the door.

"I know," I finally responded, squeezing Carmen's hand. "And I won't let them take anyone, never again."

Carmen's face split into a wide grin for a moment . . . but it didn't hide the sad flicker behind her eyes.

"Well, no time like the present," Carmen said, pushing open the doors.

I thought about my world, hoping beyond hope that time was moving slowly enough there while I was in Zafa for me to figure out what was going on and keep my family safe from La Sombra, El Baca, and whatever the Pariguayo was. Pues, Carmen was right, there was no time like the present—for all I knew, there might even be no time at all.

FIFTEEN

AT THE END OF THE Hall of the Galipotes, the four powerful, ageless shapeshifting sisters waited for us. Maria Teresa and Dede stood to the left, while Minerva and Patria stood to the right. The hall was lit with floating hot stones, the orange light almost seeming to breathe in sync with me as I walked slowly, scanning every inch of the intricate silver carvings that covered the walls nearly top to bottom.

Nope, not this part, I thought, squinting at a stretch of the carving that showed two ciguapas punching a Cucito right in its slobbering face. Which was awesome, pero not what I was looking for. I continued to search for the eyeless face from my vision among the carvings.

"Pilar." Minerva's voice echoed along the hallway.

"Welcome back. Please come closer so we can get a look at you!"

I straightened up briefly and did a perfect ciguapa salute, right fist over left shoulder just like Carmen had taught me.

"Umm, it's very good to see y'all too!" I tried to smile but it slipped into more of a grimace. "Well, not very good . . ."

"We get your point," Dede reassured me. "Pero it also—"

"Seems that you may have your own mission to discuss since you're clearly so distracted." Patria raised an eyebrow and fluttered her huge silver-and-black wings anxiously.

"Well, yes." I resumed scanning the left wall as I spoke slowly, like I was tasting the words. "But I also have a lot of . . ."

It just had to be here; I knew it had to be. Unless the carving I was looking for had been destroyed and never rebuilt. Pues, wouldn't that be just my luck, defeated by interior remodeling?

But then I saw something that took my breath away: a structure of white marble near the middle of the silver wall to the left. My gut lurched at the sight of it. La Blanca.

"Questions?" Minerva asked. "You have a lot of questions?"

"Oh yeah, sorry, I—why is that thing still here?" I asked, pointing at the white marble carving of El Cuco's prison.

Minerva smiled thinly. "So nobody ever forgets." Her shoulder-length curls rustled in that wind that always surrounded the Galipotes' leader. "One day there will be generations who never knew El Cuco; all that pain and suffering will only be stories on this wall."

"Pero that history is part of us, and we have to make sure people remember," Dede continued. "So that it can never happen again."

I nodded, still transfixed by the little model of the worst place not exactly on Earth. I remembered the cold hallways, the hopeless expression on some of the prisoners' faces, the way the crushing quiet of La Blanca clung to my dreams even months after I was away and safely in my world. But just then, I finally saw what I was looking for, something I'd seen a year ago but hadn't thought much about porque I had been focused on the image of Natasha being abducted by El Baca.

The carving was of a hairy man, pues like werewolf-level hairy, stuffed into a uniform of Trujillo's secret police, the SIM, that clung to his muscles. He was shaking hands with a man who I thought was supposed to be Trujillo with all the details of his ugly, bleach-rotted face intentionally left out.

But I realized now that it was not a man, not Trujillo, but a figure with no eyes, no nose, only a mouth. A fanged, slightly grinning mouth that sent the necklace of La Negra into high alert the moment I laid eyes on it.

"Okay, no disrespect, Doñas," I started, staring a hole into the wall, "but I need the full truth, entiendes? That's The Pariguayo, isn't it?"

A shiver went through the room. The sisters exchanged a glance, and even the hot stones seemed to falter for a minute so the orange light in the room leaned and flickered like a live flame.

"That's The Pariguayo, isn't it?" I repeated.

"Yes, it is. But the more important question," said a voice from the back, dry with age but still sarcastic as ever, "is where did you learn that name?"

SIXTEEN

LA BRUJA CERTAINLY WASN'T THE GIRL she'd once been in my dreams or visions or whatever they were, but the vieja still moved like she was only 300 years old. She marched quickly forward as if the word *Pariguayo* was pulling her in. She loomed over me, or at least it felt like it even though she was only a few inches taller than me. Pero before I could answer, I felt the wind knocked out of me as something collided with my chest and wrapped me up in a fierce hug. Pues, not some*thing*—some*one!*

My long-lost cousin Natasha was holding me so tight that my back popped. I hugged back just as tight. We held each other at arm's length, and I looked at her for the first time in a year. She wore a simple olive-green shirt and black shorts that came to above her knee. Natasha's face had gotten rounder now that she was finally free from La Blanca, and the shadows around her eyes were smaller, shrinking from eclipses to half-moons. Her arms were more muscled, and when I pulled her in for a dap, her palms were coarse and rugged like she'd just done eighty pull-ups.

La Bruja allowed herself a small smile at our reunion before snapping her head up to the Galipote Sisters and giving a defiant nod. Then she slowly swiveled her gaze back on me, and I let Natasha's hand fall from mine.

"Pilar Ramirez," La Bruja said commandingly, "where did you learn that name?"

"So I guess no hug for me?" Carmen grumbled, kicking at the ground with her backward feet.

"Enemies first, hugs second." La Bruja waved a hand dismissively. "Where?"

I was starting to get a little annoyed. "Pues, I asked my question first, doesn't that count for anything?!"

La Bruja's mouth opened to deliver a retort, but Minerva interjected. "Yes, that's the Pariguayo. Pero he's been gone for centuries." She flapped her wings to punctuate the point.

All due respect to Minerva, but La Negra clearly

didn't feel this dude was gone, swirling and bucking back and forth in my necklace. I turned back to La Bruja.

"Who was he? How do you know him? Y pues, if he's dead, why do you look so upset?"

La Bruja gave her signature eye roll, and for a second she looked exactly like her younger self.

"Porque two reasons: One, you tend to remember the names of your mortal enemies, especially if they're married, and two"—La Bruja glared at the sisters—"he's not dead, he's gone. And make no mistake, there's a difference."

None of this made any sense and my head swam with the words that had been said. *Pariguayo, mortal enemies, dead, gone,* but most of all, *married?!*

"Okay, I think we need to refocus," Carmen said, placing a hand on my shoulder. "Porque me and Pilar were attacked in The Above and we need to—"

"Attacked by what?" Natasha interjected.

"El Baca?" Dede asked.

"No, it wasn't—" I tried to answer.

"El Pariguayo?" Maria Teresa offered.

"No, I don't think—" I started.

"No, a woman wearing a white shadow." Carmen thumbed the bruise on her chin for emphasis.

"Then it's worse than I feared," La Bruja growled, both hands balling into fists.

"ENOUGH!" I heard myself shouting, the echo ringing off the walls. "Too many people are talking, too much is happening, and my family—" I paused and looked at Natasha. "*Our* family is still in danger porque whatever attacked me and Carmen is still out there. So someone is going to start the story from the beginning, porque we are running out of time, entiendes?"

I snarled and glared around the room at everyone. I don't know why I always gotta end up yelling about getting answers in this hall; just once can't things be simple?

La Bruja shot me a don't-ever-raise-your-voice-to-me-like-that again look, then settled into her story. "El Pariguayo was a man once, Trujillo's secret right hand. Pero he used to be nobody, just some low-ranking soldado who kept an eye on la gente. A filthy spy—Trujillo had a hundred of him. He needed to make himself stand out. So he somehow learned of our island, perhaps the stories still live on in your world, and he tried to open a portal to Zafa."

"What?!" I interjected. "How would he even—"

"He failed," La Bruja cut in. "The border between

your world and ours was cut off by El Odio since his power was strengthened by Trujillo's evil grip on La Isla. In the past, a human would have died from the direct contact with El Odio. Pero El Pariguayo survived, maybe because he had a monstrous, rotten heart, maybe just our bad luck, though it cost him his face. He became Trujillo's spy and master of the supernatural, the one who introduced him to our old friend, El Cuco."

La Bruja continued her story. "Trujillo was too paranoid to leave the island for long periods, he feared the people—or his so-called allies—would rise up against him. So El Pariguayo stepped in with . . . a solution. Using the powers he got from his contact with El Odio, he handled most of Trujillo's communication with El Cuco's forces, and in exchange he received riches beyond his wildest dreams."

"What were his powers?" Carmen asked.

"He could control silence." La Bruja spat on the ground. "The filthy spy could hide and appear out of nowhere in this haze, like a shimmer of heat, entiendes? Hard to track an enemy when they make no noise and can send blasts of silent magic from afar that could fell a thousand-year-old tree. Pero the real worry was if he got in close on you and wrapped that magic in a cloud around your head—then he would work his power and it would be like . . . like—"

"Like you were choking," Natasha finished. "As if all the noise was draining out of the world, and all your hope with it. El Cuco used to take him around La Blanca to check in on the prisoners."

I shivered at the memory of the magical prison, its walls that itched and clung to the edges of your brain.

"Beyond his power," La Bruja continued, "El Pariguayo played a role in crafting Trujillo's legend, spreading stories about how El Jefe never sweat, could call down the weather, and held court with El Diablo. He disappeared after the raid that killed all my sisters. Y por supuesto, many people fell into the oldest trap in the book, thinking he was dead. But he wasn't. A fact I confirmed while interrogating El Baca in the tunnels below the city."

"Why would he tell you anything?" Carmen's eyes narrowed, like she was trying to do calculus in her head.

La Bruja snorted, pero there was no humor in it. "People, or even demonios, say lots of things when they're dying. El Baca was formed when Trujillo and El Cuco agreed to build La Blanca. Demons are born from such pacts. Evil begets evil. But with neither Trujillo nor El Cuco around anymore, the deal is broken, so—"

"It's only a matter of time before he disappears," I said under my breath. "Unless he can find a way to bring about another pact and survive."

"Exactly," La Bruja said gravely. "And now, thanks to El Baca's confessions, I also know who betrayed the Bruja nation."

SEVENTEEN

SILENCE REIGNED IN THE HALL of the Galipotes at La Bruja's revelation. But it could only last so long.

"You never mentioned that!" Dede and Patria said in unison.

"Well," La Bruja stretched her fingers as if they were cramping, then continued, "the fact that El Baca escaped was kind of the priority in my mind, pero yes, he told me."

"Who was it?" I implored, heartbeat thudding in my ears.

"You wouldn't know her, or actually—" La Bruja titled her head to the side. "I suppose you've already met."

"La Sombra was the traitor?" I said, my mind wandering to the woman emerging from the white shadow, her hollowed cheeks almost glowing in the moonlight.

"La Sombra." La Bruja laughed bitterly. "Her name was Rosa when I knew her—"

"Back when you were training as brujas," I finished for her.

"Which brings me back to my question." La Bruja looked me in my eyes again. "Where did you learn that name?"

I shuffled my story into order and relayed my dreams of . . . Rosa to the gathered women, who watched me like hawks.

La Bruja's brows furrowed, then she nodded. "Rosa was even more of a prodigy than this one." La Bruja jabbed her head at Natasha, who nodded sadly as if she'd heard this story before. "And we were best friends and more—we were rivals, we made each other better because of how much we couldn't stand losing to the other." La Bruja sighed and stretched her palms again. "That made us sisters. Pero, she had a weakness. Rosa was headstrong, she didn't want to work with La Negra, she wanted to wield her, she wanted for La Negra to be the *source* of her own power. For years after the Raid, I assumed that El Pariguayo had killed Rosa. Pero instead they . . . *fused.*"

"They . . . what?" Carmen gagged.

"Paciencia, Carmen," La Bruja growled. "Rosa

wanted control, El Baca wanted to break through the barrier guarding the Bruja nation's base, to destroy us once and for all, and El Pariguayo wanted to make sure he was always powerful enough to save himself if Trujillo tried to betray him."

"He needed someone born with the power of Zafa inside them," Natasha cut in. "So the three struck a deal. El Baca used his connection to El Odio to fuse El Pariguayo's and Rosa's powers together in exchange for the password to the base of the Bruja nation." Natasha knit her fingers together and brought her arms down like a guillotine. "El Pariguayo and Rosa came together to form the sombra lady who attacked you."

"She goes by Raiza now, apparently." La Bruja spat out the last word. "And that betrayal, like all deals with the devil, created a demon, and this one gave birth to that infernal Bird baca that helped El Baca escape," La Bruja finished.

"Pues, we have to bring her to justice," Minerva declared, flapping her wings until she hovered just off the ground.

"Agreed," Dede chimed in. "Pero también, there's much we don't know. Pilar, you said she attacked you? Did she say why? How did she get away?"

So I told them everything about the chase, that

burst of power, and the sound rushing out of the world before I fell into my vision.

Pues, I still couldn't remember the exact words of that weird riddle Raiza had said.

What was that part about a storm? Ugh, this is why I record things! If only my memory were as good as—

"Carmen!" I interrupted my own story, pointing to the ciguapa.

"That's my name." Carmen smiled confusedly.

"The riddle that Raiza said when she was attacking us—how did it go?"

Understanding bloomed across Carmen's face.

"The Sweatless One approaches. Soon the seas mock the skies. Soon the howl that shook the world se regresa a la isla." Carmen squeezed her eyes shut and thumbed the bruise on her jaw. "The tide is already churning around you, little bruja. Soon the storm, then the world, everything will be as it was. What was agreed to must be maintained. The world you love is already a memory."

When she finished, the only sound in the hall was the sisters rustling their wings as we all thought through the riddle. Y pues, if it hadn't been quiet we might not have heard Natasha. Porque all the color drained from her face, and her eyes stared off into the distance as she said in a voice barely above a whisper:

"Trujillo; the Sweatless One is Trujillo . . . They're trying to bring El Jefe back to life."

EIGHTEEN

IF SILENCE IS THE ENEMY then it was in danger, porque the hall exploded with noise. Trujillo? Back from the dead? What kind of zombie apocalypse was this? It couldn't be, it shouldn't be, it wasn't fair.

"The girl's right." La Bruja grimaced. "El Baca is trying to save his own butt by forming a *new* pact with Raiza to bring back Trujillo and keep himself alive. And apparently one betrayal wasn't enough for Raiza."

"If Trujillo came back . . ." Maria Teresa's mouth creased.

"It's never been done," Patria countered.

"That's not the same as impossible," Minerva pointed out.

"We need a plan," Dede offered.

"The plan is that we prevent it," Minerva and La

Bruja said at the same time, and then stared at each other with surprise before La Bruja continued.

"A resurrected Trujillo would make El Cuco look like an insect, well . . . like more of an insect. The Pariguayo was just a foot soldier, but the rotten energy in his heart allowed him to be infused with enough power from El Odio that he became Trujillo's most powerful spy. Pero a Trujillo whose spirit has just been marinating in El Odio for years? With *real* powers of his own? The command he would have over both worlds might make him unkillable. We need to strike now."

"But strike what? We don't know where they are," Dede said.

As those three went back and forth, I looked at Natasha. She'd been quiet since figuring out the riddle, but now her whole body looked like it was shaking, and nobody had noticed. I slipped my hand into hers and squeezed as though my own heart wasn't trying to jackhammer its way to freedom.

The necklace full of La Negra buzzed and hummed against my neck.

"We don't know where to find Raiza, and we don't know how to stop her." One of the sisters argued with a scowling Carmen, who had waded into the debate.

"But La Negra does," I shouted, and everyone

turned to me like they were expecting a speech. "La Negra has been trying to tell me bits and pieces of Raiza's life, where she is, her plans, all of it. I think there's still a connection there, and we can use it to track her down and stop her before she resurrects Trujillo or hurts my family."

I expected someone to interrupt me, pero nobody did.

"Pilar is right." There was no quiver in Natasha's voice, no tremble in her hands that talked and cut the air to ribbons like Mami's. "And I'm going with her."

NINETEEN

NATASHA LOOKED TOTALLY DETERMINED AS she stared defiantly around at everyone, daring them to say she couldn't go.

La Bruja was the first to speak. "Guess stubbornness runs in the family." She gave a humorless laugh. "I'm coming too. I've been waiting a long time to take revenge for what Raiza did to my sisters."

Natasha shot La Bruja a strange look. Pues, it only lasted for a glimpse, and everyone besides me either blinked or missed it. Not an angry look, pero not pleased either. De verdad, if I didn't know any better I'd say Natasha was warning La Bruja, or pleading with her.

"I think that decision may have to wait." Minerva

cocked an eyebrow and raised her eyes. "Because normally, Fina only tries to listen at the door this long if she also has something to report."

"Huh?" I wheeled around and saw the doors of the hall gracefully swing open. A shorter ciguapa strode forward with a hasty salute first to the sisters, then to Carmen. Fina, the youngest member of the ciguapa strike team I'd led on the raid of La Blanca, looked only a little older than me. She now wore a green streak in her mane of pitch-black curls and a silver stud piercing above her left eyebrow.

"If you let me go out in the field on more missions, I wouldn't have to listen in—"

"Josefina—" Carmen whisper-shouted at her.

"Fina," Minerva interjected as she cut off what looked like it was finna be a very well-rehearsed speech by the most prodigious ciguapa spy since Carmen. "The message . . . if you please."

Fina flushed as she remembered who she was talking to and did a quick salute. Carmen rolled her eyes and pinched the bridge of her nose. "Xiomara sent word that she has spotted El Baca near the ruins of La Blanca. She requests further instruction and possible apprehension assistance."

"Why would you not lead with that?!" I asked, mad confused.

"Well, you were in the middle of a meeting! And the meeting was just getting good!"

"You are being trained in the needs of the city so one day you can be invited to meetings like this," Carmen groaned, and pinched her nose again.

"Although, obviously, the preference would be to have *fewer* meetings about the end of the world . . ." La Bruja slid in.

"Pues, they must be moving into position to do whatever magic is going to release Trujillo," Natasha pointed out. "It looks like we're going to need a bruja on both ends, so maybe La Bruja should go with Carmen to confront El Baca, and I can go with Pilar to handle Raiza in her world."

"And what if Raiza outmatches you two young brujas?" La Bruja exchanged that same look Natasha had given her earlier.

"None of our options are perfect." Minerva's voice was firm, gaining momentum and power at the thrill of finally meeting the enemy head on. "But this is the best plan available to us."

"You're not my commander," La Bruja growled, but

she looked at Natasha a third time and stood down. "But fine, you win. However—I'm serious, you'll need more than your natural abilities and a plucky attitude if you are going to beat Raiza."

"Well then, maybe we can try to bring on one of my visions—find a weakness?" I said. "Preferably without me passing out or getting hit in the face."

La Bruja's eyes didn't leave Natasha, who stared back with her jaw slightly on edge. "Yes, we'll go do that now, Pilar. It would be a shame if one of the few brujas left with The Sight could only use her ability when she's getting knocked around."

"Agreed," the Galipote Sisters said in unison.

In the silence that followed, we could pretend for a moment that we hadn't just begun the fight of our lives.

TWENTY

THE LATE AFTERNOON SUN SHONE gold as I exited the Hall of the Galipotes alongside Natasha and La Bruja.

"Okay, rookies, let's lay this all out and get started," La Bruja huffed, unslinging a bag from her shoulder.

She spread out a tarp in the sun, dropped three small, tightly wrapped packages at different points, and weighed down the edges with smooth black stones.

"Pues, what's in the packages? Ritual stuff?" I asked.

"Ritual?" La Bruja scoffed. "Mijita, this is our lunch."

"It's what?!" My head snapped up.

Natasha cocked her head to the side and said nothing as La Bruja shrugged. She sat with her legs crossed, pulled a silver pocketknife from her belt, and sliced along the package. The smell of rice and roast pork shoulder flooded out into the clearing. Against my better instincts, my mouth watered just a little. La Bruja jabbed a silver-ringed finger at each of the remaining packages.

"Look, kid," La Bruja said calmly, passing me the knife. "The work we have cut out for us is not going to be pretty. Whatever anybody says, we really might lose this one. If we're going to make it out of this"—La Bruja was deadly serious as she popped a piece of pernil into her mouth—"you'll need every advantage, we'll need every advantage. You try and save the whole world by yourself and burn out porque you forgot to eat, you're no good to anyone. And tapping into The Sight is key. Now eat."

"I understand," I said, biting into the pernil and rice, my mouth filling with the second-best pork I'd ever had.

I chewed the meat, feeling it melt and make me dream of my world, my house when Mami is cooking the pernil, steam rising from rice until the bulbs that light the kitchen waver in the heat like candles, a prayer three days in the making.

I felt a tug of guilt, eating something so good when my family was still in danger.

La Bruja stretched both arms wide, a small bottle of La Negra's black sand in each palm. "Okay, now we can get started." La Bruja turned to Natasha.

"Just like we practiced?" Natasha asked.

La Bruja nodded curtly, as if she was mad at Natasha for something.

Pues, what was going on with those two? I thought.

But before I could press the thought further, La Bruja spoke. "The important thing is that we maintain contact through La Negra. Now you"—La Bruja jabbed a finger at me—"are going to be running point on this, you're the one with The Sight, so I need you to focus on Raiza."

I steeled my jaw.

"All right, Intend a connection of La Negra from your hand to mine, then do the same with Natasha. Once the ring is completed I need you to think *only* of Raiza. If she's set foot somewhere that La Negra knows, we'll see something."

"And if we see nothing?" I heard myself ask.

"Well, then Raiza has even more time to work her plan . . . so if we don't see her, what happens next probably rhymes with *death and destruction*, porque *death and destruction* rhymes with *death and destruction*," La Bruja said, a bitter smile cutting across her face.

"Got it, no pressure."

"You'll pull it off, Prima." Natasha threaded her fingers in my own. "No doubt."

"No doubt." I Intended a thread of black sand to each of the other brujas in the circle and felt my vision go black.

Think of Raiza. Think of Raiza.

I felt a dark pulse around me like I was in the belly of a storm cloud.

C'mon maldita, where are—

The darkness rippled. I could see figures moving on the other side, pero they were blurry, like La Negra was getting bad reception.

Okay, well mejor que nada, pero I need to know where El Baca is and—

The static thinned to show the massive dog bounding through El Bosque de las Tormentas, the images flickering to black every couple of moments only to bounce back even clearer. Then a flicker again, and for a blink there was the image of the once-pristine, horrifying white tower of El Cuco's prison, La Blanca.

WEPA, finally some answers for us! Actually, wait, can y'all hear me? Natasha? La Bruja?

Pero nada. I guess when I was using The Sight like

this they couldn't speak to me. Pues, maybe I was just asking the wrong way. Maybe it just takes practice, but either way I still needed to find Raiza.

Cmon, think Raiza thoughts. I focused harder on the ex-bruja.

Raiza thoughts . . . um what are those? Storms? Trujillo? Bad dentistry? Betrayal?

The pulsing dark twisted and swirled before me as I felt my mind zoom forward. When I opened my eyes, I was staring out of Rosa's face again and saw a small squad of brujas trekking through the woods.

"All I'm saying, Miranda, is if they're fighting with El Odio's power maybe we need to adapt." Rosa's voice is clear in my ears as she looks up into the trees, scanning for danger.

La Bruja is slightly older than she was in the last vision. She shakes rain from her much-shorter locks and rolls her eyes. "To what, you being in charge?"

"Miranda." Rosa stops cold and catches La Bruja by the arm. "We can bring *her* back."

"I can't hear about this again. Cielo is gone, and we just need to accept it." La Bruja pulls her arm from Rosa's grip and turns to leave, but Rosa grabs her arm again.

"I'm telling you, all we need to do is—"

"I said drop it." La Bruja's voice is all iron.

"Don't you know I miss her too?" Rosa takes a step forward.

La Bruja's expression curdles, and she takes a firm step toward Rosa. "We don't use that kind of magic, you know that. It's not the Bruja way!"

Rosa slams her fist against the tree beside her. "So what? We just keep on as we've been while they pick us off one by one? They have the numbers, and you know it. How many more battles do we have to lose before we—"

"Accept your genius? Let you brilliantly guide us to use the tactics of our enemies?" La Bruja says, coldly appraising her longtime rival. "I wonder: Do you truly miss her? Do you want her back? Or do you want to be the one to *bring* her back?"

Rosa's face prickles with heat, tears pooling in the corners of her eyes only to be stolen away by the rain. "You can't tell me you think this is what Cielo would want." Rosa's voice is barely louder than a stage whisper. "We can win this war together! Everything can be like it was. Come with me."

"Come with you where?" La Bruja laughs bitterly.

"I don't know, anywhere that isn't here." Rosa scowls in frustration.

"I won't abandon our people, that's final."

"*I'm* your people too, Miranda!!" Rosa's fury blooms in her chest. "The trap is closing around us. Either you see that and live, or you don't, and you die."

"If only you hadn't . . ." La Bruja trails off, biting her lip and turning to leave.

"Go on. Blame me. Say it out loud for once."

La Bruja's eyes are hidden as she turns to leave. "I don't blame—" She sighs. "Cielo would have been ashamed of everything you're proposing we do to bring her back. To use the enemy's magic to what . . . resurrect her? You're so obsessed with growing your own power you've forgotten who we are."

"You have no idea what Cielo would be ashamed of! Because she's not here. Because you're too afraid to bring her back. The enemy stole all that 'we are one Bruja nation' tontería from us the day they took her." Rosa's voice is growing distant.

La Bruja's voice is icy as she turns to leave. "If the Bruja way could be stolen from you so easily, then they should have left me Cielo."

Rosa's vision stutters before me. La Bruja's words

hang between the two of them. And the vision shifts before me, revealing the image of a tear-streaked face— Cielo's face.

Rosa flinches backward as if she's just been punched. I feel her mind flood with Cielo's face, dirty and bruised, a little cut brimming with blood down the middle of her lip.

Rosa begins to walk forward, toward the ghost of a voice at the edge of hearing growing louder with each step.

"You promised, Rosa," Cielo cries. "You promised."

Rosa stops in her tracks, palms on either temple as if she means to squeeze the voice from her head.

Promised. Promised. Promised.

Rain falls fast and cold, peeling the full color of Rosa's memory back and leaving only darkness behind. Rosa's eyes shoot open as she roars in pain and slams her hand into a small tree trunk, the bark fracturing like a mirror. *Promised, promised, promised,* comes Cielo's voice again. As the rain grows colder still, thunder layering over thunder, Cielo's voice is next to Rosa, and I am staring out at a different memory.

TWENTY-ONE

IN THE COLD BARRAGE OF the rain, Cielo's voice is a mosquito at the base of my neck. "Are you sure this is a good idea, Rosa?"

"Cielo, mijita, maybe you're too inexperienced for this mission? Because we can go right ba—"

"No no no, I want to help the ciguapas!" Cielo says to Rosa. "I just think maybe they should, like, also know we're here."

"Look, we've been following orders for hundreds of years, and it's only led to defeat. Maybe it's time to make some choices of our own. And if the ciguapas come across the Pariguayo without any bruja backup? They're toast. So that's where we come in. With or without Miranda."

"Pues, we'd be heroes!" Cielo's voice glows with pride.

She's still too young. Tu lo sepas, she doesn't belong in the field at that age. I hear Miranda's voice echo through my head.

I squeeze my eyes against the rain. *What does* she *know? If she's so smart, how come we're losing the war?*

Pero just then a sharp, dry smell enters my nose. I feel my face curdle.

"Cielo, do you smell smoke?"

"Smoke?" Cielo's voice is a whisper. "More like wet dog."

The revelation hits me just as the first claw from above misses by inches. I roll, pulling Cielo with me as the second claw smashes the bark to splinters.

I chance a glance over my shoulder. It's just as I feared; El Baca himself got the drop on us—literally, porque the mange-ridden beast launched himself down from above.

We turn to find higher ground. El Baca roars, and the sound of the rain is drowned out by the flood of Cucitos and the high screams of a legion of bacas.

"What do we—" Cielo's question is cut off as the heavy remains of a branch explodes above our heads. I feel a cut open on my forehead, the rain diluting the blood that's rising to the surface, sharp and hungry for the air.

"Survive," I growl through gritted teeth.

I drop through a gap in the ancient branches. I hang there, the wood cracking beneath El Baca's heavy gait. Just as he passes over me I explode back up and Intend a stream of La Negra at the beast's ankle. But I miss by inches.

A second later, El Cuco's filthy servant wheels around to face me.

I show no fear. "You're shorter than the stories say," I spit, casting La Negra around me in a coiling sphere of grains.

El Baca's eyes narrow, all his muscles rippling beneath his matted black fur-like smoke. He wastes no time, easily tearing a branch the size of Cielo from a tree and hurling it at my feet.

I backflip away, but the beast is already closing the gap. One of his paws slams the breath from my chest. As I fly backward, I Intend La Negra out in two thick ropes, slinging my body forward and driving one of my boots into El Baca's chin.

I land on my feet on a branch in front of me, but I quickly have to hit the deck as Cielo has Intended La Negra into—wait, what?

Pues, it really is a set of huge fists, one over the other, doing everything in their power to slap the ash from El Baca's mouth. I glance at Cielo and can tell this kind of casting is taking everything she's got.

This is no time for glory, this is a time to escape.

I hurtle toward Cielo and snatch her around the waist, the way I did when we were girls. Before the long war, before the first home burned, and the next, and the next. Back when we were a nation who moved when we wanted, where we wanted, not a group of glorified fugitives, brujas with no home but the one the enemy hasn't yet turned to ash.

"And. Take. That. Payaso." I hear Cielo hollering in my ear, heavy in my arms. Too heavy.

Grains of La Negra shower around us, rain among rain, as we hurtle closer to the ground. I try and swing us upward to safety, but, amid the thunder, I aim for a branch and miss—the ground rushes up to meet us.

Pain slams through me, ribs squeezing the breath from my body as soft white lights pop behind my eyes.

I smell ash in the air before the first Cucito launches toward us. Cielo's eyes are wide, searching for escape. Bacas pour over every root in El Bosque, like a wall of smoke.

"Cielo!" I call out, fearing she'll be overrun. But the

little bruja wipes blood from the corner of her mouth and stands.

"I'm good; are we regrouping with the ciguapas or . . . ?"

"No, this must have been a trap for them, let's—" An idea flashes in my head. There just might be a way out of this.

"Umm, Rosa . . ." Cielo's voice quivers.

"UP!! We have to get up as high as possible. GO GO GO!!" I holler, and there's shades of Trainer Nina in every syllable.

Cielo nods and casts twin cords that zip her into the air. I follow, chasing the rain to the clouds.

We skitter over branches as the roar of the pursuing enemy fades below us. Good thing bacas can't climb.

Well, most bacas anyway.

Just as I predicted, the maldito looms out of the shadows—teeth first. El Baca roars as he follows us up the tree.

I was right! I shout in my head, triumph briefly pouring honey over the dread in my stomach. *If we can just get him up high enough, maybe we can get him to fall* hard. *That'd be a story that'd make this all worth it. I'd be the bruja that killed El Cuco's right hand. I'll be a—*

And just like that, my dreams snap in half right before me.

El Baca's paw seizes Cielo's ankle. The whole world slows as my hermanita tries to shake the monster loose. But his palms are huge, and she can't twist free.

Not like this. I half whisper. I'm reaching for the bottle of La Negra at my waist, but Cielo has plans of her own. She directs a huge blast of La Negra directly in El Baca's jaw, and he yelps, falling backward and taking Cielo down with him.

"NO!!" I cry out, Intending La Negra around my hand into a set of long claws that tear away chunks of bark in the tree nearest me.

Cielo and El Baca tumble through branch after branch, my hermanita's face a mask of pain. Finally they hit a branch thick enough to slam the breath free from her chest, and I hear a sickening crunch. El Baca slides off just as I land heavy next to Cielo.

When I manage to get Cielo turned on her back, I see one of her feet is twisted backward like a ciguapa's. There's no way she can run on that.

The cries of Bird bacas thicken the air around us like heat. And there's no way El Baca will stay down for long.

We're trapped.

Cielo groans as she stares at her shattered ankle, every line in her body tense and alive with pain.

"I could carry you," I lie, but Cielo shakes her head grimly.

"Then we both get caught. I can't let you—"

"Well, *I can't* just leave you here!"

"No." Cielo's voice is old steel, weary but still sharp. "You promised. No captures, death before chains."

"Cielo . . ."

"You. Promised," Cielo says again. "Just . . . make it quick, huh?"

El Bosque comes alive with light, the thunder hot on its heels.

No no no no. There has to be another way.

But the shrieks of the Bird bacas are growing. I try to haul Cielo up onto my back, but she cries out in pain at the motion.

"Rosa." I expect Cielo to scream, to plead, to curse me again and again, but her voice is soft. "You promised not to let them take me alive."

I stare at my hands, willing La Negra to a point, a blade. Something quick. But my hands stay bare. I feel the blood thudding in my ears, trying to wrench the sand into something, anything that will let Cielo join the ancestors. But La Negra will not come, no tumbao in my blood, . . . just silence dancing in my veins. I scream, slamming the bottle at my hip to the ground and watching the useless grains of black sand dust the air like ash.

From within Rosa's mind, I watch the next part of the scene playing out in stop-motion. Her hands feel like my hands, pero I have no control over them.

I can only watch in horror as Rosa slowly pulls a gleaming silver knife from her boot. Her grip on the knife's handle bleaches the color from her knuckles. She stares at Cielo's anguished face and almost gently pulls Cielo toward her in an embrace, a last hug between sisters, as the knife finds its mark.

A second later, Rosa lets the knife handle slip from her fingertips. Blood blooms across Cielo's chest, an island of red just below the heart.

The life starts to leave Cielo's body. And I want to scream, to unmake this memory. But then a malevolent whisper steals my attention away. "I think that's enough for one day."

I wheeled around and saw Rosa—no, not Rosa, but *Raiza*, pitch white with fury. A vision within a vision. There was a cold glare in her eyes, and I felt a viselike grip on my shoulder. The scene melted to inky black-ness around us.

"I . . ." I began, my own voice hoarse and distant, as if I hadn't spoken in days.

Pero Raiza wasn't tryna hear any of it, entiendes?

"Doom is coming, Pilar Ramirez. There is no memory that can unmake the inevitable. And I am inevitable." Raiza's lips curled into a smirk.

"Inevitable, huh? Pues, all dictators really have the same playbook." I smirked back at the vision of Raiza.

"Insolent child, you have no idea."

"Neither did El Cuco. Then he met me," I shot back. "Like I said, all dictators have the same playbook, y también they all fall the same way." I stared at Raiza, unblinking. "They just make different sounds when they hit the ground."

Raiza scowled and slashed her hand down, the darkness shattering around me.

TWENTY-TWO

I FLUNG MY EYES OPEN, shocked by the light. The land around me was dry, the rain in El Bosque centuries away. I felt Natasha's warm hand slide into mine as I settled back into my body.

"Well, you must've seen something she *really* wasn't planning on revealing." La Bruja smiled grimly, holding out a bowl of pernil.

"What happened?" I asked between mouthfuls. "Weren't you there too?!"

"Me? No, not after that tontería in the jungle." La Bruja cut a mean side-eye, grimacing at the memory of her and Rosa's conversation. "You were flying solo from there."

"So you didn't see—" I started, then bit my lip, not wanting to mention that I just saw Rosa kill her and La

Bruja's mutual best friend. It could be mad triggering to just drop that on her, war or no war.

"No. I suspect when Rosa merged with El Pariguayo, her connection to La Negra was fractured. But a thin thread still remains. And so with your Sight, you can conjure glimpses of her past and present."

"If only I could break into her memories without her knowing I'm there," I muttered.

"You fell deep into that memory, and, just as I suspected, she felt your presence and intervened."

Without another word, La Bruja summoned strands of La Negra from her flask and formed them into a flat disc on which stood two figures.

"I think a demonstration will help explain how this works." La Bruja jabbed her hand at the smaller figure. "The short one is you."

La Bruja continued to shape La Negra, forming tree-like roots on the bottom side of the disc that connected the short and tall figures standing on the top.

"There's a connection between every bruja and La Negra, as you well know. Y pues, try all you want, it's never all the way gone."

One of the connecting threads between the figures of me and Raiza pulsed below the disc and the taller figure, Raiza, shook noticeably. I reached my hand out to the root connecting the two of us, and the warm sand braided itself around my wrist as the Raiza figure on top of the disk wrenched violently.

"So if I pluck a chord of her memory here," I said, tasting the words, "it creates a ripple in La Negra where you can see where Raiza is hiding. Like I literally struck a nerve?"

La Bruja gave a small golf clap.

"Yup, and it got her. Hook. Line. And sinker." La Bruja couldn't help a note of pride in her voice.

"She's gonna be big mad now." I twisted my mouth. "She looked furious."

"Well, look at the bright side." La Bruja put her calloused hand on my shoulder. "She already wanted you dead, so nowhere to go but up in that relationship."

I let out an ugly snort laugh which Natasha caught as well. Then a moment later the gravity of the situation settled back over us.

"Was that conversation you had with Rosa the last time you ever saw her?" I asked La Bruja.

"She disappeared right after that. We thought the Pariguayo got her." La Bruja gave a strangled laugh. "Back then, I thought I knew what loneliness was."

Natasha reached a palm out, but La Bruja eyed it warily and carried on with her story.

"You've faced Raiza, pero you didn't know who she was. Now you do. She's always been selfish, she's always been obsessed with her own power, y también she's always been terrible at staying dead."

I nodded.

"Given the tremors I felt in La Negra when she threw you out of her memory, Raiza's somewhere in your world now. If you get a chance to finish her off for good—take it. There's no other way."

TWENTY-THREE

"SO WHAT WAS THAT LOOK between you and La Bruja?" I asked Natasha on our way over to Dilcia's workshop. We'd been instructed to pick up my machete and get ready to stop Raiza from ending the world and bringing back Trujillo.

"Oh, what look?" Natasha blinked as if she'd just noticed the sun.

"The one where you were trying to get her to not come with us back in the hall . . ." I said slowly.

"Ay Pilar, no me molestes," Natasha said with an almost believable giggle. "Who do you know who has power to make her do anything?"

Pues, points were made. Still, my gut told me Natasha wasn't telling me everything that was up, and it put me in an even worse mood than before. I was about to try asking a follow-up question, pero we arrived at Dilcia's workshop, and Natasha was already pulling open the door.

"Well if it isn't my two favorite brujas!" Dilcia said warmly through a mouthful of pastelillo. "My bad, Tomasito dropped these off this morning." She wiped a crumb from her mouth.

"No hay problema!" Natasha waved off the apology. "Honestly, I was going to ask if you have extras."

"Do I have extras? Pues, that little boy drops off ten every morning. He wants me to train him as an armorer. ¿Para qué? ¡Quien sabe! He knows the war is over, well . . ." Dilcia grunted as she looked at us. "Mostly over, but yes there's a basket full of them. The darker shells are chicken, the lighter ones are kind of a vegetable mix."

I gagged involuntarily at the vegetable mention, pero Dilcia just shrugged her shoulders and laughed.

"He's got quite an eye for flavor, that boy. He told me what was in them once, and it shouldn't work, pero it does." Dilcia grinned widely. "Anyway, Tomasito's pastelillos are not the only gift I have for you!"

Twin blades sat on Dilcia's workbench, a pair of

silver fangs. I picked up the one engraved *Catorce* and felt its warm and familiar weight in my palm. It moved fluidly through the air, like it was part of my arm. The edges were lined with La Negra herself. I felt the faint tumbao of La Negra as the blade danced.

I hadn't realized how much I missed the blade until it was back in my hands. Pues, I had really hated leaving it here in Zafa.

But I've lived with Mami way too long to think that I could've snuck a magic demon-killing machete past her. Some things are even beyond the powers of La Negra, entiendes?

The second blade was almost identical, but where the handle of mine was made of metal and leather, this one was constructed from rosewood carved with intricate patterns, the inscription on the blade reading *La Mariposa de Dos Mundos*.

Natasha stared at the blade with awe as Dilcia handed it to her. I sheathed my machete and grabbed one of the chicken pastelillos out of the basket. De verdad, Tomasito might have a much better future folding dough than folding metal. It was almost as good as Abuela's.

Dilcia turned to address Natasha. "I carved the

handle with a knife from your original world; the blade and, of course, La Negra came from Zafa. When you go up there to stop that backstabber, you'll have a little of both your worlds in every swing."

"It's perfect." Natasha's eyes were shining. "I love it!"

"Well, hopefully it brings you back here safe. I still think y'all should have a ciguapa squadron for backup." Dilcia grinned, and the ciguapa's gold tooth winked.

"Uh, you'd probably stand out." Natasha held her blade up to the light, admiring the effect.

"We're the epitome of stealth. We are trained from a young age in the art of misdirection and combat," Dilcia said boastfully.

"All of your feet face the opposite direction, though," I pointed out, checking the sheath on my machete one last time. "Pues, I feel like that's the main problem."

"Some say problem, some say genetic advantage, pero I'll just follow the orders and wish you both good luck."

Dilcia gave us a ciguapa salute and then pulled Natasha in for a fierce hug.

"Make sure you come back to us, muñeca. I hope your old world loves you as much as we do."

"I guess we'll find out," Natasha said, sheathing her blade.

Half an hour later we met with La Bruja and Carmen at the edge of Ciudad Minerva, and they brought a surprise guest with them.

I hadn't seen Minerva outside the Hall of the Galipotes since the last time a circle had gathered to send me home through the Olvida paper last summer.

"You're coming too?!?" I asked, eyebrows flying up my face.

"No, I need to stay in Zafa and prepare to unite my powers with my sisters in case El Baca's plan comes to threaten our city. But, I wanted to see all of you off."

"One last time?" La Bruja half grinned, but there was no humor in it.

"One *more* time," Minerva responded. "I don't know how, but I believe we will win."

"Why?" Natasha asked quickly, then clapped her hand over her mouth.

We all stared, and Natasha slowly lowered her hand from her mouth.

"Pues, it's not that I believe we won't win, pero . . ." She trailed off.

"Because we have before," Minerva said, a gentle breeze drifting through her hair. "We've won before, and once you know that, what else is there to believe?"

I hadn't known I needed to hear that. I don't know if any of us had, honestly.

"Well, let's go and stop that bleeding then," La Bruja said, lightly punching Carmen's shoulder.

Carmen had been strangely quiet up until then. Pero the ciguapa pulled me deep into her arms without a word. Anybody ever hold you so close that you don't really hear them talking, you just feel the vibrations of each word in your bones?

"I never got the chance to fight for my family." Carmen's voice hummed against me. "No matter what happens up there, I'll be down here fighting for yours to my last breath, hermanita."

I hugged her as hard as I could, pero I didn't know what to say. Even after everything, the situation was so huge and heavy. It was starting to settle back in my mind that I didn't know how much time had passed in my world. Raiza may have already won.

Pero Carmen wasn't done. "You brought me back my family, we can do this."

"And you gave me back mine." I grinned at Natasha

before turning back to Carmen. "And now you are my family too. I'll see you again soon."

Carmen gave that mischievous grin. "True, nobody's ever rid of me."

"Least of all me," grumbled La Bruja. "Nos vamos! Before El Baca summons something else along with Trujillo. And you." She pointed at Natasha. "Recuerda, keep breathing, kid."

Natasha nodded, her mouth a grim slash as she checked the buckle on her machete.

The last thing I saw before me and Natasha stepped hand in hand onto the Olvida and rushed back toward our world was Carmen and La Bruja, rushing toward the edge of theirs.

TWENTY-FOUR

OKAY, SO I KNOW I said earlier that just once I wish I could do a little interdimensional travel without getting sand in my mouth. Pero it turns out sand isn't always the biggest problem. Por ejemplo, the minute me and Natasha emerged from the Olvida, ready to try and save the world, all of these things happened:

1. There was a massive crack of thunder beyond the window of Prof. Dominguez's apartment.
2. The doorknob to my bedroom started to jiggle.
3. I shoved Natasha into the shower and made a signal to hide.

I didn't know who was on the other side of the door, but I did know that whoever it was thought

Natasha was dead and had been for fifty years. And me and Natasha were in kind of an apocalypse-related hurry and didn't have time to explain where she'd come from.

I leapt onto the bed just in time for Mami to come through the door with a broad smile in the middle of her perfect, unharmed face. Pues, for a minute I forgot to be afraid, that danger still threatened my family.

She was all right, Mami was alive.

Between the ticktack percussion of the rain, I heard a small gasp from the shower. Mami started to squint toward the shower, but I interrupted before those special Dominican mom instincts kicked in and she could be sure something was up.

"Hey Mami, sorry about earlier . . . in La Zona, I mean. And for any texts I missed, I been umm . . ." I drummed my fingers as I looked for the right words.

"It's all right, Negrita, we all get a little too hot sometimes. Pues, one time in July it got so hot I could have sworn I saw la ciguapa herself, can you believe it?" Mami laughed and flicked her wrist like she was shooing the joke out the door. "Anyway, I wondered if you would want to join your vieja madre in a game?"

I bit my lip. Natasha and I needed to get out there and find Raiza. The necklace full of La Negra was humming so hard. Pero I couldn't tell Mami that without telling her about Zafa, and I couldn't tell her about Zafa without telling her I was a bruja, and I couldn't tell her that without telling her about Natasha. Y pues, part of me really did want to tell her, pero it was only going to slow us down more to explain everything.

Mami's shoulders slouched, and her grin slipped. She lowered the box of dominoes I realized she was holding. "Never mind, mija, I should let you rest."

"No, Mami I—"

"It's fine, pues you might be too young to remember this, pero your father loved to play dominoes on rainy days. It's how we met." Mami sat at the edge of the bed, the dominoes clicking against one another inside the box as she cut the air with her hands. In her palms, the dominoes sounded like the world's shortest rain stick. "All the men at the panadería didn't want me to join, pero your Papi was the one who mixed the dominoes y también he had the most careful hands I'd ever seen. I wish . . ." Mami sniffled and wiped her eyes.

Over her shoulder, Natasha peeked her head out from the shower to stare at Mami for the first time in fifty years. I tried to make eye contact, jerk my head back toward the shower, pero Natasha was transfixed.

"Can I tell you something?" Mami asked, without asking. "Cuando it was time for me and Abuela to sneak out of this place, I had to go first, alone, without her. I wore these long velvet gloves, and they flew us out in the middle of the night. Pues, I stayed that whole first night in America in the airport, afraid to fall asleep porque I barely spoke the language and I didn't want to miss my next flight. After Natasha—I wasn't sure what might happen to our family.

"I wish your papi could have lived to see the woman you're growing up to be. Y también." Mami took a deep rattling breath. "I know I lost Natasha, pero sometimes, mija, I swear she was reborn in you, entiendes?"

Mami squeezed my hand, and I could smell her slight coconut scent and the little salty layer of sweat.

I shot another quick look over Mami's shoulder. Natasha had resumed her hiding in the shower, though I could have sworn I heard a sniffle.

It looked like Mami was finna say something else, pero at that same moment another four things happened at once:

1. A crack of thunder shook the walls.
2. Something huge and wet slammed into the

shower window, and Natasha slipped, yelped, and spilled out onto the ground.

3. Mami saw Natasha and froze before quietly fainting back onto the bed, spilling dominoes everywhere until the noise competed with the rain.

4. My phone buzzed, and out of instinct I looked and saw that I *had* missed something after all.

TWENTY-FIVE

**Mysterious Storms Ravage Three
International Cities**

(Madrid, Spain) Onlookers in three cities across the globe were stunned earlier this evening after cloudless skies devolved into a series of chaotic storms that are baffling meteorologists in San Cristobal, Dominican Republic; Paris, France; and Madrid, Spain.

The news alert's headline flashed behind my eyes as I knelt at Mami's side with Natasha, who was shaking Mami's limp hand like it was an on switch.

"Grecia, Grecia, I'm so sorry," Natasha exclaimed, pero Mami was totally knocked out. "I didn't mean to scare you, I didn't mean—"

I put my hand on Natasha's shoulder to try and calm her. "Tranquilase, Prima. We gotta keep it down or Abuela and Lorena are gonna pass out just like Mami and they'll be sitting ducks for Raiza and El Baca. We have to get Mami comfortable, then slip out, can you do that?"

Natasha got a steely look in her eye, then took a deep breath and squeezed Mami's hand one more time before nodding. "You're right, pues, what was that thing you were looking at earlier anyway?"

"What? This?" I said, holding out my phone to her. "It's what phones look like now."

Natasha looked at the phone and weighed it slightly in her hands with awe in every line of her face. She clicked a few buttons then wordlessly handed the phone back to me. I had a bad feeling the rest of that article had something to do with our mission to stop Raiza, so I read it aloud for Natasha.

While reports are still coming in from all three locations, the storms appear to have some commonalities that baffle researchers, climate change experts, and storm historians in equal measure. Eyewitness reports and videos confirm that each storm has been characterized by rain with a rusty, blood-like hue that has sparked some false reports that it is raining blood. While anxieties about blood rain

are unfounded, this coloration is unprecedented, as is the
sudden nature of these storms. They appear to be almost
spontaneous, as weather conditions in Madrid, Paris, and
San Cristobal were supposed to be clear the entire week.
Could this be a function of catastrophic climate change?
For further information, I contacted—

I stopped reading porque something about the location of the cities was tickling my brain. Pues, what was connecting those three places?

"It's the Curse of San Zenon," Natasha said, fluffing the pillow she had placed under Mami's sleeping head.

"The what?"

"De verdad, La Bruja knows a couple of things about the magic of El Odio and one of them is the curse of San Zenon. Before either of us was born, there was a horrible hurricane that killed six thousand people and El Jefe took advantage of that chaos to make himself leader of the whole island before most people even knew what was happening. Those places the storm is hitting, do they have anything to do with him?"

I racked my brain porque I could almost put it together—then finally it clicked. Back in La Zona, Dr. Vega had mentioned that Trujillo didn't have just one grave!

"It's all the places they buried him!" I said as another wave of thunder rolled over us. "The Trujillo family moved his body twice porque they were afraid his graves would be, like, desecrated or something."

"Pues, if I had been here, they would have been." Natasha's eyes were steel. "Raiza is definitely behind these storms then. She must be trying to re-create the hurricane of San Zenon by combining the three storms. If they all come together and make landfall on Santo Domingo, he'll be free."

"And we'll be doomed." I slammed my hand into my fist and kicked at the ground, sending several dominoes spinning into the opposite wall as a fork of red lightning outside blasted the room with crimson light.

"How did you find her before?" Natasha asked.

"I didn't, La Negra did," I said, uncorking the necklace and letting La Negra flow along my arms in her intricate pattern. "I don't think Rosa's connection to La Negra was severed all the way, and La Negra is seeking her out. Pero I don't actually know how to use The Sight, it just kinda . . . happens."

I closed my eyes tight and tried to feel around for that special tumbao that played along my skin when me and La Negra were in conversation, but it still felt ragged and fuzzy, like trying to stream a movie on a

3G network. I felt my pulse pounding in my ears and my whole body prickling with heat. I held my breath and tried to push toward the feeling again, my connection with La Negra, and this time I saw something, heard trees brushing against each other, not yawning under the winds of the storm. Pero just as quickly, it was gone. I groaned in frustration and beat my hands against my thighs.

"Ugh it's no use! I can't get a grip on the tumbao for some reason."

Pues, of course everything was falling apart right now. I felt a hand on my shoulder and unsqueezed my eyes.

"It's not you, it's the storm," Natasha said softly, half her face in shadow, half in scarlet glow from the red lightning sizzling in the distance. "Raiza's storms must be interfering with La Negra. Pero I think if we work together, like La Bruja taught me, we can figure out where she's hiding. I can show you how the magic is done."

"And what if it doesn't work?" I fought the tremor in my voice as the feeling of my brain soaking in ginger ale tripled.

"Then we make for the eye of the storm. Pero we go down swinging, entiendes?"

She stuck her arm out and I clasped it at the elbow. La Negra hummed as a power surged between us that made every pore on my body feel like it had a tiny light pushing its way out. The black sand spread from my arms and combined with the grains of La Negra Natasha had brought in a green flask. La Negra formed a circle around us, and I felt a new, faster tumbao moving through us both. Without another word, we each reached out and touched the pulsing circle of La Negra, and I forced my eyes shut, searching for anything that felt like the Pariguayo, like Rosa, hoping against hope we weren't too late. And when I opened my eyes, they were Rosa's again.

TWENTY-SIX

EVERYTHING I SEE OF ZAFA through Rosa's eyes is a lush whisper. The branches of the trees of El Bosque yawn and sway lazily. I feel the heat of a mostly windless day, the sweaty, clingy warmth of rain that falls straight down. There is no thunder as Rosa tosses a small silver knife up and watches it spin until it glints in the half-light, whistling down like an arrow, before catching it by the blade between two fingers like it's nothing. Pues, besides that it is so quiet you could forget this is a war memory.

"Dios santificado, how much longer?" Rosa says to herself. "That Cucito squadron was supposed to be through here a while ago."

She tosses the knife once more, and it whistles like

the opening notes to a song. It has long, sad notes that cut off when Rosa catches the knife.

"And this Pariguayo, quien sabe when we'll see him." Rosa tosses the knife higher this time. "What kind of useless strategy is 'listening for his quiet' anyway?"

Rosa doesn't even look as she catches the blade again between her fingertips. The knife swings into the sky, spinning so fast that it is no longer a handle and a blade but a small flashing planet, a moon that would cut if you touched it. It finally lands, sinking into the tree branch she crouches on without making a sound.

"Carajo—" Rosa starts and scrambles backward, pero it's too late.

At the end of the branch, near the trunk of the tree stands the Pariguayo, his face featureless and smooth and white as a pearl aside from his smirk. A heat haze surrounds him, and only the Pariguayo is in focus in its center. He wears long tan pants and a short jacket over an olive-green button down with a slight gap at the collar. His head is perfectly bald, not even stubble. Y también his skin doesn't look like skin, and the waxy effect of it is mad creepy, entiendes? It's like someone carved him out of an evil candle.

Rosa's frantic eyes shoot between the Pariguayo's face, the knife, the surrounding trees. The maldito seems to know he has the upper hand. He flicks his wrist, and his smirk stretches slowly into a crooked, half-melted smile. Slowly, the sound bleeds out of the trees and the patter of the rain fades to nothing until all I can feel or hear is Rosa's heart, slamming against her ribs, begging for escape from the Pariguayo's suffocating silence magic.

Rosa's gaze settles on the Pariguayo just as another rhythm forms along her arms—the tumbao of La Negra, fighting her heartbeat for dominance. The Pariguayo raises a hand without a word, pero Rosa has already dropped beneath the branch. In the blink of an eye she Intends a stream of La Negra around the branch and launches herself back up to close the distance. She lands soundlessly and finds herself face-to-face with her enemy, who swings a backhand at her as she lands. Barely missing his fingers, she rolls to his left and kicks him with all her might in the ribs. Without missing a beat, she Intends the grains of La Negra into a set of claws on her left hand and clings to the trunk of the tree.

The Pariguayo is pissed now, his mouth a thin, lipless slash. Pero he doesn't even grunt when Rosa lands that kick on him. He isn't used to being hit, but he is definitely able to give as good as he got. He raises his hand and shoots something that looks like a cloud of heat haze at Rosa, who moves to dodge but is caught on the shoulder and sent spinning to a lower branch where she lands on her knees.

Pero Rosa isn't ready to give up so easy. She explodes forward without a word, the claws of her La Negra–infused left hand dragging along the branch, willing the branch to split beneath the weight. Y pues, if I hadn't met Raiza, I would have thought Rosa had the Pariguayo dead to rights. She's mere inches from the Pariguayo's face when he jumps up and almost glides to the branch of a nearby tree, dodging an uppercut of La Negra that would have torn the demon in half. Instead, he simply stares from the next branch like he's studying her.

Rosa grunts and takes a deep breath, her nose filling with the wet moss scent of the silent rain all around them. Then she feels the first muffled crack beneath her feet and sees that the branch, thick and sturdy to the point that it must be hundreds—pues, maybe thousands—of years old, is splitting down the middle. Rosa leaps with all her might to the branch the Pariguayo still silently watches her from. The branch she escaped, which is the size of a small school bus, peels away from the tree and falls toward the ground, exploding into a hundred pieces without making a sound.

Rosa is quick to flip herself up onto equal footing

with the Pariguayo. With a furious snarl she reaches for the flask of La Negra that was on her hip but realizes with a gasp that it's no longer there. The Pariguayo has no eyebrows, pero his waxy skin shifts upward like he's raising an eyebrow in mock surprise.

Pues, I think, *that's checkmate.*

The forest around us sputters briefly, and for a moment we aren't in El Bosque. Beyond the Pariguayo I see ships—ships from my world churning in the water, a bright fork of red lightning over the blackened ocean. It looks familiar, pero it only lasts a moment before the memory flickers back to the past. The rain falls soundlessly around Rosa as a pulse hammers in my ears.

And for the first time, the Pariguayo speaks.

His voice is terrifying. It sounds like there are many voices echoing inside a tin suit disguised as a man. Pero, de verdad, none of that is as scary as what he actually has to say.

"You're exactly what I've been looking for."

Again the world flickers behind him, and I see those churning and rocking ships, a massive rust-colored fortress lit by red lightning. And just as quickly, it disappears.

Pues, what am I supposed to do now? Where is this place? And why does it feel so familiar?

Rosa snarls and charges, only to be sent flying

backward by another shimmering cloud of silence catching her in the chest.

"Pues, that's on me for thinking you'd realize this fight is *over*." The Pariguayo's many voices peak and grunt as he sends an even larger wave of silence at Rosa that catches her around the head and stays there.

The inside of Rosa's head feels like being in an airplane that never stops pressurizing itself. The air seems to be pressing through her temples and into my own. Pero that doesn't help with breathing. It feels like suffocating, and the shimmering cloud of silence gets more and more opaque until all I see is gray smoke.

Just when I begin to wonder what happens to you if you suffocate in someone else's flashback, the Pariguayo yelps and releases the cloud, and Rosa spills forward, coughing and spluttering, her eyes cloudy with tears as she looks up. And despite everything, I feel Rosa's satisfied grin between coughs.

The Pariguayo clutches the side of his face as if he's been touched by a hot poker. Rosa pushes herself back to her feet and I realize that she still has a few of her claws from La Negra clinging to her fingertips, and she'd sent one at El Pariguayo as the silence choked her. La Bruja had really not been kidding when she said Rosa was a prodigy.

I feel a flicker of sadness in my chest—Rosa could've been so much more.

"Maldita bruja." The Pariguayo's voices shake with anger as he peels his hands from his face to reveal an inch-wide burn, a perfect circle where his left eye would be if he had one.

"More where that came from!" Rosa shoots another two of the five remaining claws at the Pariguayo, pero the Pariguayo flicks his wrist, and I watch in horror as the grains of La Negra bleach and fizzle to the ground—just like they did opening the doors of La Blanca and when Raiza froze my attack in midair back in Santo Domingo.

"I will put you down if it's the last thing I do, monstro!" Rosa yells, ready to charge again, but El Pariguayo merely holds up a hand. And when he speaks, his voice is cold.

"*Monstro*," El Pariguayo says, "is just a word, like *evil*, that the weak made up. It's just a word, a name, a lullaby for the powerless."

Rosa jabs another claw of La Negra into his ribs, and he howls again but doesn't release his grip. The edges of Rosa's vision begin to dim, tunneling on his waxy face, his cold, misshapen mouth.

"I want to help you," El Pariguayo continues.

"Surely, little bruja, you must realize your cause is doomed."

Rosa kicks at the Pariguayo, who hurls her backward into the trunk of the tree, sending all the air rushing from our lungs.

"You place your faith in a glorified hourglass, bruja, and look: Without her you are nothing."

Rosa reaches for the tumbao again and then pauses, considering his words.

"Haven't you ever wanted more?" the Pariguayo continues. "To know everything you're capable of? To not be tethered to a power that controls *you*? To not continue to do the bidding of a woman who stifles your potential and treats you like a child?"

Rosa swirls back up the top of the branch, and in seconds La Negra is a blade at the Pariguayo's throat. Pero Trujillo's favorite lackey doesn't even flinch his waxy head.

"Aren't you tired, Rosa, of being nobody?"

Rosa freezes and her eyes widen. "How did you—"

"I've been watching you for months now," the Pariguayo says calmly. If the blade of La Negra at his throat bothers him, it doesn't show at all. "You should know, your 'sisters' who came with you on this mission are already gone."

Rosa grabs the Pariguayo by the collar and pulls him even closer to the blade of La Negra swirling along her hand.

"You're all alone porque you were the most powerful," the Pariguayo continues, unfazed. "You were the one I revealed my voice to."

"I'm honored." Rosa's voice drips with sarcasm.

"You ought to be." The Pariguayo shrugs. "I've seen what you're capable of." He gestures at the splinter that used to be the branch they were fighting on. "And you've seen what I'm capable of. Imagine what we could be together, away from all of this . . . imagine the power you could have in The Above."

Rosa's arm lowers a small amount, but she keeps the blade trained at the Pariguayo's throat.

"There's no La Negra in The Above," she says carefully, like she's tasting the words to find the lie.

The Pariguayo spreads his hands. "When you separate yourself from that child's weapon, you'll be surprised what's possible, mija. Pues, now you could kill me here where I stand. The war would go on without me, your island would keep receding, and you and your fellow brujas would all die one day or another porque that *sand* you built your faith around is dying. I know you can *feel* it."

Rosa takes in a shuddering breath, and I feel my pulse in my ears.

"You get to decide, Rosa." The Pariguayo spreads his hands again. "Do you want to be the last bruja, or do you want to be a god amongst mortals?"

Pues, just because you see the ending coming, just because you heard about it over and over again, doesn't mean it hurts any less, entiendes?

I watch in horror from the inside of Rosa's body as the tumbao slows to a crawl and stops, as Rosa lets the last grains of La Negra slip from her fingertips, as she pulls her arm back.

"I'm listening," she says calmly as the tree rattles with muted thunder.

"NOOOOO!!!" I heard myself screaming, so hard and from so deep within me I barely noticed it was the first time I'd heard my voice in what felt like hours. I pulled my eyes shut tight and continued to scream again and again. I screamed until there were no words left, just a massive storm of grief, and when I finally opened my eyes again, the last of Rosa's memory had been whipped away, and I stared out from Raiza's eyes at Calle de las Damas, atop Trujillo's palace, daring the storm to dance.

TWENTY-SEVEN

"THE PALACE!!" I SHOUTED BREATHLESSLY to Natasha as I tumbled back from the vision, La Negra buzzing heavily against my chest. "She's at the palace, calling the curse down. We have to stop her."

Natasha grabbed at my shirt to steady me. I felt my nausea and dizziness ease as the tumbao melded with my heartbeat and slowed my pulse.

"Okay, but how are we going to get past our family?"

As if on cue, I heard the weirdly formal way that Lorena always knocks on my door: three quick taps and then two slower ones. Lorena, a weirdo even at the end of the world. Pues, we just couldn't catch a break.

"Just a second," Natasha offered, then clapped a hand over her mouth.

"Ughhh," I groaned as Lorena knocked a second time, harder.

"Hermanita? Mami? Whose voice was that? Are y'all watching a movie without me?"

"Umm . . ." I scanned the room for an excuse; the last thing we needed was Lorena trying to tag along to the apocalypse brewing in La Zona Colonial. "Sorta?"

Now it was Natasha's turn to glare at me. Sue me, there was a lot going on!

"I'm uhh . . ." I continued to sputter. Pero then I saw the camera! ". . . showing Mami a new cut of the documentary I was working on!"

"In the middle of the storm?"

I cringed. "Private screenings happen rain or shine!"

Natasha gave me a look and jabbed her head at the window above the shower, and I understood immediately what she meant.

"So yeah, we'll just use headphones, sorry to disturb you!"

"Umm, okay, but . . ." Lorena said, pero I was already easing Natasha out of the window, and I followed a couple seconds later, ready to make a break for La Zona until I realized . . .

"Ay por favor," I groaned. "We didn't get you ciguapa gloves from Dilcia before we left Zafa."

Pues, how were we going to make it to La Zona now if Natasha couldn't climb from building to building? You can't call an Uber to the eye of the storm; no tip is worth driving *toward* blood-red lightning!!

"Oh, that's not a problem." Natasha spread her fingers as grains of La Negra poured from the flask at her hip. "I've got a few tricks of my own."

I raised an eyebrow as Natasha Intended La Negra into two long ropes. She cast them out to a neighboring high rise of apartments and went zooming up into the night sky.

My jaw dropped. But I recovered quickly and followed, using my gloves to launch myself after Natasha, who was nailing her Spider-Man impression as the storm boomed around us.

After about fifteen minutes of flying across the Santo Domingo skyscape, though, the taller buildings got farther apart, and a bolt of red lightning tore the sky open. I saw Natasha glance down, searching for her next handhold, when something made her freeze mid-swing. Everything slowed as I ran along the roof of one of the shorter buildings. Natasha's braids of La Negra flickered and came apart and she began to fall, hands around her throat, down toward the ground.

"NO!" I hollered, summoning La Negra on instinct and casting a black rope to grab Natasha around the waist and haul her back. The wind rocketed us back and forth as I held Natasha against my chest, y pues, it didn't look good. Natasha was flailing in my arms, breathless, desperate like a fish pulled into air for the first time.

I propped Natasha against an air-conditioning unit on the roof and scanned around for Raiza. Could she have sent one of those clouds of silence?

Thunder boomed above us again as Natasha seized my hand and squeezed until I felt a sharp pain between my knuckles.

"Ouch, Natasha, what the heck?" I snapped at the pain. "What's wrong?"

"Volkswagen," Natasha said back. She fought to sit up, pero I squeezed her hand back from inside the vise grip she had on my left hand. "No time to explain. Have to stop. Storm. Just."

"Natasha," I said, shocked to hear some of Mami's steel in my voice. "I don't know what's going on, pero you can't fight like this."

"Leave me, then," Natasha wheezed, still fighting for breath.

"Never." I squeezed Natasha's hand again and her fingers eased a bit as she looked into my eyes, wide with fear. Pues, what was it La Bruja had said before we left Zafa?

"Just keep breathing, kid?" I said, unsure.

Natasha took a deep breath and eased her grip on my hand so my blood came rushing back in pins and needles.

Three deep breaths later Natasha pushed herself shakily to her feet. I looked over her head, y pues, if it wasn't clear before where the storm was coming from, it was now. The dark clouds had begun to swirl and churn above a spot off in the distance.

"I was outrunning one of Trujillo's Volkswagens when El Baca came for me," Natasha said, flexing her fingertips. "I saw one down there, and every day I was in La Blanca I thought, *If I could have just not gone to the colmado*—I just . . . lost focus. I'm sorry."

I swept her into my arms and held her fiercely. We stayed like that for a minute as she shook against my shoulder before holding me at arm's length, wiping the rain from her eyes.

"Okay, I think I'm ready."

"You sure?"

Natasha cracked the knuckles of both hands as lightning turned the whole city crimson above us. She smiled as she said, "Yeah, let's go kick her butt and save Zafa; it's in my blood after all."

TWENTY-EIGHT

WHEN WE ARRIVED AT LA ZONA it was everything and nothing like it had been earlier that day. Pues, I couldn't even believe it had only been *one* day, pero there me and Natasha were on Calle de las Damas, staring up at Trujillo's former palace. Dark clouds spun overhead, slowly draining into the nest of lightning sparking in the storm's gaping eye.

"I don't know why they call it the eye of the storm," I said as we both stared up at it in horror.

"It's more like a mouth," Natasha agreed, and flexed her fingertips as grains of La Negra settled along her arms. "Si, pues, esta vaina fea—the mouth that'll swallow the world, entiendes?"

I tied my hair back as I nodded, then drew my machete.

"So what's the plan?" Natasha asked, thumbing the sheathed machete she'd strapped to her back.

"We go up and kick her butt, storm stops, no resurrection, no demon dictator," I said, trying to sound confident.

"You make it sound so easy." Natasha rolled her eyes.

"Subtlety is for before the apocalypse, machetes are for during," I said, preparing my hands in a basket. "All right, on three I launch you up there. I'll be right behind you, and maybe we have the element of surprise and get the drop on her."

Without another word, she ran at me with her jaw clenched, a determined look in her eye as thunder boomed again like the whole sky was a cannon.

"Well, so much for counting to three," I grunted as Natasha timed her jump, her foot landed in my outstretched palms, and I rocketed her up to the top of the building.

She floated above everything for a moment, her long curls splayed out behind her like the tail of a comet. Her hands were already reaching for her machete. Pues, Natasha had been many things in Santo Domingo: a daughter, a cousin, a threat—y también, now outlined against the storm that might end both of her worlds, she was the Mariposa, a warrior, a bruja. I felt a weird calm watching her. Natasha was no longer the quivering, thin-limbed girl I'd rescued from La Blanca, not the raven-haired desaparecido from Mami's tear-stained photographs either. She was something else now, and for the first time I thought no one could stand against us.

I got a grip on a window ledge and hauled myself up by the edge of the building just in time for Natasha to land on my left, one knee to the ground. We both glared at Raiza, who hadn't heard Natasha's bad-ass entrance. We had the element of surprise, and it appeared luck was finally on our side . . .

And then we heard a scream. An inhuman scream from near the eye of the storm, and I swore I saw a pair of wings, briefly illuminated before disappearing again.

Raiza wheeled around, one arm still raised to the storm, her waxy face contorting into a snarl as her eyes flicked between me and Natasha, calculating her odds. Her face seemed even thinner than before, her eyes bloodshot, and her cheeks were so hollow it looked like her head might implode. Pero then she straightened a bit and smoothed her strangely dry hair away from her face, her scowl replaced with an amused smirk.

"You're too late." Raiza grinned sharply, the shadow of the Pariguayo's voice echoing across her own as if she were hollow inside.

"RAIZA!" Natasha howled above the storm. "Stop this, you can still redeem—"

"I do not seek redemption, but power!" Raiza shot back, thunder booming behind her as I scooted to the right, trying to get out of her line of vision. "And I understand things about power you could only have dreamed of in that cell."

Natasha's whole body tensed, pero she didn't flinch.

Raiza continued her monologue. "El Cuco was weak. Even his lapdog didn't have the power to overcome a simple teenage girl and a washed-up old hag."

Natasha's hand flew to the machete's handle at her back. She flicked me a look and stayed in position as I crept two more paces to the right, out of Raiza's sightline. Pues, it wasn't fighting strategy, pero if I've learned anything from watching the Bulls it's that two-on-one is always easiest if they can't see you both at the same time, entiendes?

"The Sweatless One approaches, can you hear the song now? I have done things death herself couldn't imagine. And I wanted you to see it all firsthand." Raiza's free hand balled into a fist, and without even glancing my way, she sent a swirling cloud of her silent magic right at me. "I will finally wipe this pathetic world clean."

TWENTY-NINE

SO MUCH FOR THE ELEMENT *of surprise.* I rolled to duck Raiza's no-look attack as Natasha charged forward.

Raiza dodged the stampeding girl and bent backward to avoid the whip of La Negra I Intended toward her, one arm still tethered to the storm above us.

"Is that all from the heroine of Zafa?" Raiza taunted, sending another wave of suffocating silence that Natasha barely dodged.

"Oh my god!" Natasha grunted, closing the distance between her and Raiza, both hands on the hilt of the machete. "Do. You. Ever. Stop. Talking??" She punctuated each word with a swing of the machete.

Raiza glided away from every potential blow, dipping and dodging as fluidly as a dancer before finally leaping back from a cut that nearly separated her nose from her face.

"I haven't had anyone but these filthy humans to speak to in what feels like millennia." Raiza cracked her neck to either side. "Every day the powerlessness of this world demeans me, y también—"

Pero Raiza never finished that sentence, porque I had just shot a blast of La Negra that caught her right in the chest and sent her sprawling across the roof.

"Natasha," I called over the storm. "I figured it out—she stops talking if you hit her!"

The storm bellowed in response, the eye swelling with scarlet light as we again heard that scream from above, inhuman and everywhere. A series of images from La Negra flickered behind my eyes: *wing, fire within a beak, two smoldering red eyes.* Pero there wasn't time to think about what was above, porque Raiza was scrambling to her feet, free right hand clutching her chest, and the other already back to unleashing the storm.

"Okay, my turn," Raiza said, and without any warning she spun in furious circles, sending out rings upon rings of silence magic.

"Oh, you have got to be kidding me!" I leapt over wave after wave of that horrible magic, feeling it so close to my body I got that same nausea I'd had in the vision of Rosa's fight with El Pariguayo.

Natasha was also caught up dodging the rings of deadly silence as they spun out faster.

"We'll never get close enough to beat her at this rate." Sweat from my forehead mixed with the rain, stinging my eyes.

Pero just then Natasha proved why Trujillo had been so afraid of what this little bruja could do that he called in demons from another world just to make her disappear. Natasha leapt up moments before a thick ring of magic could sweep her ankle and directed a blast of La Negra at the ground. It raised her high above so she hung suspended in the air like she'd just jumped off a trampoline. Thunder shook the whole island, and time seemed to slow. Raiza's eyes flashed as she looked at Natasha.

Still hanging in the air, Natasha sent a long stream of La Negra that lassoed around Raiza's outstretched wrist. Raiza's eyes went wide, and she released an agonized scream. Natasha yanked and zipped forward as if she were on a Jet Ski and soon buried both feet in Raiza's chest, barreling her over as the two wrestled for dominance.

The storm swayed and bucked over us as I summoned La Negra to me and launched Natasha's fallen machete into my outstretched hand. I charged over to where Natasha had managed to land again on top of Raiza, briefly winning the power struggle. Raiza's waxy face was a mask of pain as she slammed a bony fist into Natasha's ribs, making her gasp but not release the hold La Negra had on Raiza. I lowered each blade to either side of Raiza's neck as she glared at me.

"You cannot stop what has begun," Raiza hissed at us, twisting and curling like a snake as she looked me in my eyes. "Did you think this was all a coincidence?!"

"End the storm." I grimaced and held the blades closer to her neck.

Pero then, she started to laugh—the kind of laugh movie villains use before they reveal there's a bomb in their headquarters.

"The great heroine of Zafa comes to the island just in time to see El Jefe return." Raiza grinned coldly. "The unbeatable Pilar Ramirez, the future of the brujas, the fraud savior comes to La Isla. You can't think fate is still on your side."

I flexed the blades again, pero a new cold sweat was breaking along my brow. Natasha summoned another cuff of La Negra for Raiza's other wrist, and the ex-bruja bellowed in pain and hideous laughter.

"Seems like fate's on our side from where I'm standing," I said, trying to force my voice to sound confident.

"I heard all the stories of how you were going to be the greatest bruja who ever lived. And I spent a year plotting, porque I wanted to witness the moment you realized you couldn't win. So here it is." Raiza's grin was wide and bloody as understanding began to dawn on me. "Yes, yes, the remarkable Pilar Ramirez comes to La Isla on an all-expenses paid trip . . . with her family. A free trip that seemed to *magically* appear out of thin air."

The dread started as a shake in my arms, the twin blades of the machete quivering with the reflection of Raiza's wild, cruel grin blossoming in each as she said:

"Yes, with her entire family. What was that charming phrase you Americans love so much, Negrita? Something about birds of a feather?"

THIRTY

THE WAIL OF THE BIRD baca I had first encountered in Zafa pierced the sky.

Natasha's focus cracked, and the tethers of La Negra fell from Raiza's wrists, leaving behind ugly burns. A massive bolt of red lightning slammed into La Plaza, sending cobblestones flying everywhere. More lightning churned down from the sky, breaking the ground below and smashing a tunnel to . . . somewhere.

A second later, I glimpsed the ruins of La Blanca through the newly formed tunnel. Just our luck—it led directly into Zafa.

"Well, that's my cue." Raiza smirked. "I've got a storm to finish, so buena suerte."

And in a cloud of heated mist, Raiza was gone.

Perfect, she'd inherited that power from the Pariguayo too. Just perfect.

Pero there was no time to worry about that porque there was another ear-splitting scream from above. Me and Natasha watched the Bird baca slice out of the storm. Panic flooded through my body as I thought about what a baca, especially El Baca's personal pet, might do with Mami, Lorena, and Abuela. They were sitting ducks if we couldn't get back to the apartment and rescue them. Or take The Bird out first.

Pero what about Raiza? I thought, still staring at the spot where the ex-bruja had been only a second before.

Raiza must have gone back to Zafa to finish the curse. So we had a loose baca going after my defenseless family, a magical hurricane hitting three cities at once, y también the villain we were after had just disappeared. Oh, and if we couldn't stop all these things in time, the world would be plunged into darkness by a resurrected Trujillo.

Worst. Summer. Vacation. Ever.

The Bird baca was already on the other side of the square in the middle of La Zona. Natasha screamed her frustration, pero even her scream was swallowed by the thunder of the storm. My pulse was doing double time in my ears, a tumbao with a deep bass that I realized a second later wasn't just my blood, but my own feet. Before I knew it, me and Natasha found ourselves running in lockstep toward the edge of the building and after The Bird. What good was saving the world if we lost Mami? Pues, she was my world.

"I've got an idea," Natasha gasped, clearly winded, as we neared the ledge of Trujillo's palace. "Pero I need you to trust me."

I looked at Natasha and nodded, focusing on breathing and keeping pace.

Natasha closed her eyes and whispered something to herself under her breath before her eyes flew open. "Okay, I need you to slow down a bit, and when I signal, just hold your arm forward."

As we reached the ledge of the building I slowed half a step to let Natasha take the lead. I glanced up, scanning the sky for any sign of The Bird, pero the rain was coming too thick to see—or it was too far ahead of us. Pues, what I would've given for the ability to fly just then.

Speaking of which, I looked to my right and saw Natasha summon another whip of La Negra between her palms, her legs almost a blur beneath her. The coppery smell of the rain was sharp in my nose as my eyes widened. Pues, call it cousin telepathy, bruja instinct, pero I knew exactly what Natasha was about to do as she Intended the rope of black sand toward me the same way she'd Spider-Manned her way across half of Santo Domingo. I caught it with my free hand.

I whipped forward, gripping the rope for dear life as a stream of images flashed through my mind: El Bosque shaking like an earthquake was running through it, a cyclone carving through the white waters that surrounded Zafa, a huge and yellowing set of fangs. And then I was up, flying forward at dizzying speed. Pain lanced through my ankle as I landed hard on the roof of the next building. Pero nothing was going to stop me. I gritted my teeth and rolled forward, La Negra settling along my arms as I heard a thud that could only have been Natasha landing beside me. And just like that we were running again, the dull pain in my ankle marking every step.

There's no pain, there's no pain, there's no pain. As we neared the edge of the next building that thought ran through my head over and over until it was almost a chant, almost a prayer.

I Intended a thought to La Negra and felt the tumbao increase in tempo as me and Natasha both cast out black sand ropes like fishing lines, catapulting ourselves forward. Pues my heart was in my throat, but I wasn't about to let Mami get hurt. Nothing was stopping me from taking that Bird down. We zipped over alleyways and the drone of motorcycles we couldn't see. Each jump and swoop pulled us harder forward, zooming until finally Natasha saw it first and breathlessly shouted to me.

"To the right, te veo?"

And there it was, that demonic Bird shooting forward like an arrow. I didn't hesitate, calling La Negra back to my hand only to send a bolt of the black sand at the beast. It missed a wing by inches. The Bird baca wheeled and gave an inhuman squawk, coal-red eyes savage above the cruel, gray curve of its beak. The Bird dove, screaming toward us, and in its throat pulsed a red light like an engine.

"I think we got his attention." I grinned through the pain and planted my feet.

Pues, sue me, I joke when I'm nervous. Plus Natasha laughed, so now I know it's a family trait!

The Bird dive-bombed between me and Natasha as each of us rolled to the side. Natasha's machete was drawn, pero The Bird was already rocketing back up into the sky to make another run at us.

"You got any idea how to fight a bird?" Natasha asked.

"No, pero I know how to kill a demon . . . same principle, right?" I quipped as a roar of thunder announced The Bird diving back toward us.

Natasha swung her machete in a heavy arc, pero The Bird was ready for it and spun at the last minute to glide under the blade. It screamed at the blade, and a wall of sound slammed against us. I closed my hands over my ears. Natasha's machete glittered in the dim scarlet light of the storm as it spun out of her hands and sank, point down, into the other end of the roof. The Bird glided past us again.

"Okay, that flying thing is really starting to piss me off!" Natasha spat, and summoned La Negra into a pair of whips.

"Nah, we need a new strategy—we gotta stop letting him split us!"

The Bird was circling us now, plotting his next move.

Me and Natasha stood back-to-back and summoned La Negra into a protective circle around ourselves. Despite how terrible the situation was, I felt a warm sense of calm as our powers flowed together. Pues, this was what the bruja's mantra had meant. No matter how bad things got, we were partners, and we were one. A warm, golden feeling pooled in my chest, and the coppery smell of the rain melted away. We waited for The Bird to attack again.

"You said you knew how to kill a demon?" Natasha said at my back.

"Yeah," I said, calculating as The Bird passed out of my sightline and into Natasha's. "They were never birds, though."

"Well, how do you kill a demon?" Natasha asked as I heard the screech of The Bird, signaling it was about to attack.

I reached my palms out, reshaping our protective ring so armlike tendrils formed around the magical dome.

I lashed out at The Bird with one of the tendrils, but it wheeled away just in time to avoid the strike.

My hands were a little full, so rather than speak to Natasha, I felt along our connection through La Negra, the shared tumbao a clear chorus, Intending the shape of my plan to Natasha like telepathy. Her mouth split into a wolfish grin, a warrior's smile—like I said, this girl was 100 percent pure Ramirez!

"Yeah, let's try it!" Natasha called out, cracking her neck and scanning for The Bird as it gunned toward us again, its beak wide open like it was about to devour us.

I rolled out of La Negra's protective circle, which rippled, as Natasha was now the only one maintaining the connection. But she was ready.

Natasha waited until the exact minute the Bird baca was about to turn toward me to seize each of its ash-gray wings with a tendril of La Negra. The Bird roared in pain, pero only for a minute, porque Natasha wasn't done yet. She used both tendrils to slingshot The Bird toward me, and I felt a spray of heat and ash rain down over me as the demon Bird's throat caught on my machete, and it gave one last clawing scream and disappeared forever.

Pues, like I was meaning to say, you kill a demon the same way you kill anything else: by taking its head.

THIRTY-ONE

"PEW." NATASHA RETCHED AND SPAT on the ground. "I think some of it got in my mouth."

I flicked the ashy remains of the Bird baca off my machete's blade and sheathed it before yanking Natasha's out of the ground and handing it to her. More thunder rolled over our heads as huge holes in the clouds opened above the Presidential Palace. Pues, I'm no expert, pero everything in me told me that could only be a bad sign.

"We need to get back to Zafa," I said gravely.

"What about Grecia?" Natasha asked, sheathing the machete at her back. "What if Raiza has more bacas going after her?"

"I don't think she does." I was surprised by how confident I sounded.

"How can you be sure?"

"Porque Raiza thinks she's won already. She's always been arrogant, too sure of herself. I think she wouldn't have expected to fail."

"Either way, the Olvida paper is back at the apartment, isn't it?" Natasha pushed a loose wet curl out of her face.

"Actually . . ." I pulled a folded sheet of paper from my back pocket. "I snatched it just before we left. Just in case . . . well, pretty much this happened."

I scowled back in the direction of the Presidential Palace. Natasha's eyes widened as she considered the Olvida in my hand.

"Good thinking," she said, her mouth creasing as she touched the page and found it was unnaturally dry despite the rain. "I don't like this, pero this is what we have to do."

"I don't like it either," I said, laying the page on the ground between us, Mami's confused face still at the front of my mind. I wasn't ready to let that be the last time I saw her face. Losing wasn't an option. "We're gonna have to go Game 6 Jordan to have a prayer for this one."

"We're gonna have to what?"

"Right, forgot you weren't around for that reference. Never mind, the point is we *have* to win this fight."

I took Natasha's other hand, and we slapped our palms down on the Olvida, rushing away from the thunder-cracking sky and falling down into pure white.

When we arrived, Zafa was unrecognizable. For starters, this wasn't the stretch of beach that I'd arrived at on either of my previous trips to Zafa. The sand of this part of Zafa's coastline was still white as a fresh pair of Nikes. I put my palm to the ground and felt around, letting the bleached grains pass through my fingers in streams as Natasha did the same and shook her head. No tumbao, no black grains of sand. Wherever we were, La Negra hadn't healed this part of the island yet, and that could only be bad news for the both of us, entiendes?

Pues, at least the ocean was still pure white, pero it churned and bucked like it was trying to tear itself in two. The air was heavy with the scent of rain, but none was falling. Not near us anyway.

BOOM!!!

A wave of thunder rolled over us like cannon fire,

and that's when we looked to the north and saw just how bad things had gotten. The skies were one solid mass of crimson storm clouds, dense and shifting like a nest of snakes. My stomach turned to lead at the sight of it, pues, it was easily five times as big as the storm above Santo Domingo and funneled up from a point as if it were half hurricane, half nuclear bomb cloud.

"The curse is nearly complete," Natasha half whispered, her voice cracking. "We're too late."

"Not if we take the tunnels in El Bosque!" I said, pushing myself to my feet and nudging my glasses up the bridge of my nose. "I'd bet anything that the cloud is coming from what's left of La Blanca."

"Which means La Bruja's in the middle of that." Natasha frowned, then shook her head like she was tryna get rid of a bad dream.

I'd been so caught up watching that scab of storm clouds blooming over Zafa it hadn't occurred to me that Carmen and La Bruja must also be in the middle of it. Had they found El Baca? Or had he found them first? There was only one way to know.

Fear sliced through my chest. I'd almost lost one family in my world, I couldn't stand the thought of losing another.

Natasha and I made a break for the forest, white sand spraying out behind us in waves. My lungs and muscles burned from the fight with Raiza and chasing down The Bird. When we finally reached the edges of the massive trees it became clear something was wrong. I tried to put my finger on it as we kept to the shadows in case Raiza and El Baca had more surprises waiting for us.

Then a sickly sweet rot smell filled my nose. El Bosque normally smelled mossy, pero now every breath filled my mouth with a sour taste that made me wanna hurl. Pues, it smelled like somebody had left a trash bag full of plátanos in the sun for at least two weeks. But that wasn't all.

"It's so quiet . . ." Natasha remarked, then her eyes went wide as she stared up, holding out her hand. And that's when I realized it too . . .

"There's no rain. No rain anywhere." I stopped in my tracks, mouth hanging open.

Pues, since the first moment I arrived in Zafa, you could count on El Bosque de las Tormentas to, well, be El Bosque de las Tormentas. But as I drew my finger along the trunk of one huge tree and then another, the bark crumbled away to dust. I realized it also hadn't thundered once since we'd been inside. Raiza had stolen the forest's rain, and already it was starting to die.

I bent and plunged my hand into the dirt, searching for a sign, hoping against hope there was a tunnel.

But I felt nothing.

Just a hollowness where tumbao ought to pulse with song and memory. How would we get to Raiza in time if we couldn't—No, there was no time to think of failure, there was only now, this moment, to try and find our way.

I closed my eyes and searched once more, willing the tumbao to beat like a drum.

And then I felt it, dim music below the soil, weary but unmistakable. I dug my hand in deeper, feeling the cool, wet earth around my palm until a stream of images flooded my mind. The way through the tunnels, La Blanca collapsing, a bolt of red lightning above El Cuco's wrecked kingdom.

"Natasha, I found it!" I crowed, ripping my hand out of the soil and sending chunks of rich, dark dirt in every direction, boring a hole in the ground that led to the tunnels beneath.

I felt the tumbao sync with my heartbeat as we both jumped in.

With Natasha at the front and me at the back, we worked our arms in harmony, Intending and guiding La Negra as if we were rowing a boat down white water rapids. The black sand churned beneath us as I steered us through the maze of dead ends and wrong turns toward the storm flickering behind my eyes.

And then another image came, and my heart dropped into my stomach as a wave of heat prickled beneath my skin.

It only lasted a second, pero it seared itself into my memory instantly. I saw La Bruja, mouth bleeding, collapse to one knee before Raiza, whose eyes were wild and bloodshot. She cackled like a madwoman, a laugh that nearly unhinged her jaw.

And just like that, the image was gone, and I almost stopped directing the sand. The wave of La Negra we were riding hiccupped, and Natasha's head nearly hit the ceiling.

"Pilar, wha—"

"La Bruja's in trouble!" I shouted.

Pero she wasn't the only one.

As Natasha stared back at me, I saw her face thrown into sharp focus by a blast of light. My eyes adjusted to the light just in time to see that a muscular arm blanketed in thick black fur had *punched* through the tunnel. Before I could even scream, a huge, clawed hand wrapped its dirty yellow nails around Natasha's shirt, her eyes widening in shock, and yanked her up into the light.

THIRTY-TWO

"NATASHA!!!" I HOLLERED AS I Intended La Negra into a tidal wave that rocketed up through the hole in the tunnels.

Above, I saw what could've been a re-creation of the carving on the walls of the Hall of the Galipotes. El Baca, the hulking man-dog, was snarling as Natasha struggled to break free of his hold.

Pero like, El Baca wasn't what he'd been last I saw him. When La Blanca had fallen he'd had thick dark fur covering him head to toe, each yellowing tooth sawed to a fine point, and his arms were corded with muscle. Now the shadowy bipedal dog had long lines of fur missing, the skin beneath glimmering with sweat and gray like a fish on ice. His beady red eyes were ringed with yolk yellow, and one of his ears was bent at a weird angle like an antenna. Pues, the fall of La Blanca hadn't been kind to El Cuco's right hand at all, entiendes? And unluckily for El Baca, Natasha wasn't who she'd been when he'd last kidnapped her either.

"Get your hands off me!" Natasha cried out, swinging all her weight forward and aiming a swooping backward kick that caught El Baca squarely on the chin. He didn't drop her, pero Natasha wasn't done yet—she stuck out her hand and a cord of La Negra swam to her fingers as easily as flowing water. My heart hammered in my ears as Natasha cocked her arm back hard, slamming a whip of black sand into El Baca's bad ear. He roared in agony and Natasha tore herself free from his claws.

El Baca, bloodied and bruised and enraged, stepped toward Natasha, ready to seize her again, pero now it was my turn to direct a flood of black sand that sent him staggering back.

"YOU!" El Baca glared through his watering eyes at me.

"Well, I have been known to answer to that," I shot back, another blast of La Negra waiting at my fingertips. "Pero we're in kind of a rush."

"Oh, Baca knows," the slobbering hound snarled.

"Baca learned to listen, the drums, the drums beneath the ground. Everywhere beneath—"

"Pues." Natasha slid her machete from her back and held it out in front of her with both hands like a samurai ready for battle. "Did La Bruja hit you so hard you forgot full sentences, feíto?"

I smirked. Gotta hand it to Natasha—she's a Ramirez to the core.

"The drums drove Baca!" He snarled, flexing as some of his fur drifted to the ground like ash. "Every day, never-ending. Nowhere to go."

"Yeah, consider my sympathies limited, bestia," Natasha said coldly, and charged forward with a roar that nearly matched El Baca's.

I joined in and launched myself forward, dodging one swiping blow. Then El Baca kicked out at Natasha, driving in from the other side. The kick glanced her shoulder, sending her sprawling over a gnarled root.

"Never disappears. Never, never," Baca growled as he swung at me again and again.

I was on my heels now, trying to roll out of his way. This wasn't the cold-blooded bounty hunter El Baca had been—he was . . . *desperate*. A massive crack of thunder boomed above our heads as one of his claws sliced a sleeve of my shirt. My eyes widened as I sent a blast of La Negra at the ground, launching myself backward just in time. A split second later, a branch the size of a Honda crashed down and sent blasts of sand, wood, and dust in a huge cloud around the clearing.

"I CAN DO THIS ALL DAY, YOU MALDITO PERRO!!" Natasha hollered, both hands laced with the intricate designs of La Negra.

Gray with dust, El Baca slammed a clawed fist into the broken branch and hurled himself at Natasha. I sprinted toward the log and hauled myself up as quickly as I could, palms slick inside my fingerless gloves. A sharp pain told me I was prolly bleeding from somewhere on my forehead, but I didn't care.

Pero I only needed to glance across the clearing at mi prima to know the battle had shifted. Natasha wasn't flinching; she had a steely glint in her eyes that told me she had been waiting a long time for this rematch.

I leapt from above, drawing my machete, and slammed it down into the dirt, but El Baca dodged to the side just in time. Now on all fours, he closed the gap with Natasha and sprung to his full height, folding both his hands together as if he was going to squish her to death. Pero Natasha threw both hands up and a shield of La Negra exploded above her head, sending El Baca stumbling back from the force of his own reflected blow.

I blasted out from my crouch, machete singing in the breeze as I opened a flaming cut on the bounty hunter's exposed hip. El Baca roared in pain and frustration, smoke leaking from the wound. Natasha wasted no time, slamming El Baca with one blast of La Negra and then another. Now it was El Baca's turn to retreat. But Natasha continued to push forward, arms working furiously as if she were trying to punch clean through the beast. Not for nothing, it looked like she just might.

I tried to take advantage of El Baca's distraction by charging again with the machete, pero he saw me at the last moment and swiped a massive backhand that sent me flying into the log that had collapsed from above. All the wind surged out of my body and little white lights popped behind my eyes. I squinted, pero my head was ringing, and it seemed like an army of El Bacas was battling an army of Natashas. The Natashas screamed as they kept swinging, unleashing hundreds of years of stored-up punches and pent-up vengeance. The El Bacas snarled as they tried to dodge the storm of Natasha's fists.

A thunderclap shook the trees around us—I blinked furiously, trying to force breath back into my lungs. El Baca ducked beneath one of Natasha's blows and sprung forward, tackling my cousin to the ground. Pues, El Baca's face never really moved, pero I could've sworn he was smiling, teeth gleaming with slobber and savage joy as he raised an arm—claws ready for the kill.

I had to save Natasha.

"NO!" I yelled, now on my feet, casting a whip of La Negra that lassoed itself around El Baca's arm. I held on for dear life, digging my heels into the dirty ground. Speaking of the ground, Natasha grabbed a handful of the useless white sand and hurled it into El Baca's weepy eyes and wriggled away as the dog swung wildly.

Sweat fell down my back in rivers as another crack of thunder shook the clearing.

We have to end this soon. I scanned the ground for my machete. *If El Baca kills us, they win. If he stalls us long enough for Trujillo to return, they win, then they kill us.*

Ay el diantre, this was just perfect.

"Pilar!" Natasha called out as one of El Baca's swipes cut deep into a tree where Natasha had been standing a second earlier. Bark went spinning in all directions like confetti. "Any. Time. You. Want. To. Hop. *In.*"

Each blow from El Baca was met with another shield of La Negra. Pero the stalemate could only go on so long. The two of them were in a dance that was as much about luck as ability, each daring the other to make a mistake.

Pero El Baca already had made a mistake. Fifty years ago, when he stole my cousin out of my world and into this one. He made the mistake of messing with my family.

I spotted the gleam of the metal handle of my machete and hurled a stone at El Baca to distract him. It whistled past his ear as I sprinted to grab the knife.

"¡Ven aquí, feíto!" I crooned, almost a song, as I yanked the sword from the earth without breaking stride.

El Baca barreled toward me, a freight train of matted fur, both his eyes yellow like the pus from a scab. He was on two legs, then all fours, then two again as he closed the distance.

"You have taken everything from me!" El Baca howled, "Now I take—"

Nothing. He took nothing porque I slid like a baseball player beneath his outstretched arm. I saw a glint of silver out of my right eye. To my left stood Natasha, machete back in her left hand, ready to charge again.

"Man, he is really not taking well to unemployment!" I joked.

Natasha couldn't resist an eye roll as the demon dog bounded toward us and reared up on his hind legs, ready to try and deliver a final blow.

Y pues, a final blow *was* struck.

Natasha and I cast twin cords of La Negra which met in the middle as we sprinted low to the ground and felt the thread pull taut, sending El Baca flying forward into the dirt. We didn't waste a moment as we wheeled around and drove our machetes, at the same time, deep into El Baca's back.

The wounded demon's final howl was swallowed by the crack of thunder. El Baca unspooled in thick black smoke around the blades. And just like that, all that remained of El Baca was ash, rushing up to meet the lightning blooming on the horizon.

THIRTY-THREE

THE LAST ECHOES OF THUNDER rolled over the clearing as Natasha yanked her machete from the ground. Pues, I expected her to smile, maybe even dance, pero Natasha just lifted the blade to her nose and sniffed deeply, her expression souring.

"Sulfur," she explained.

I nodded and sheathed my machete.

The rotting stench of the dying forest surrounded us as we jogged back toward the hole that El Baca had punched above the tunnel.

"You think Raiza has other allies in El Bosque?" Natasha asked, pausing at the edge of the hole and staring down.

The pit El Baca had punched in the soil was slowly leaking white sand and dirt into the tunnels like an hourglass. My heart quickened and a single bead of blood dripped from the cut on my forehead. I wiped it away with my thumb and spat on the ground in disgust.

"Pues, maybe?" I answered. "Pero like, they couldn't be worse than El Baca, right?" But something was still bothering me. "I guess I'm just—"

"Wondering how he knew where to search for us in the tunnels?" Natasha finished for me. We both smiled in spite of the stench surrounding us.

I stared at the spilling white sand. "We don't know it won't happen again with a different enemy . . . but we don't have much time if we're going to save La Bruja."

Natasha didn't answer, pero she made a clicking noise with her teeth at the word "save." I was going to follow up on that, pero I felt a small stream of images pass over my eyes as the tumbao called us down into the tunnels. I saw my own hand, the tunnel wall, a book opening in a flurry of pages, ciguapas crouched around a fire swapping stories outside the walls of a silver Zafan city I'd never seen before. La Negra wasn't huge on words, pero this one felt pretty clear: *Touch your hand to wall, I will tell you the story of what you need to know.* I flicked a look at Natasha, who was drawing invisible symbols in the air as if she was tryna do an AP math problem.

"¿Qué?" Natasha asked, shaking her head as if she could shake away whatever she'd been imagining.

"La Negra wants us in the tunnels." I shrugged and offered her my hand.

Natasha tucked a lock of hair behind her ear and took my hand. Without another word we leapt down into the tunnels, and I touched my hand to the wall as Natasha churned the waves of La Negra, pushing us toward the ruins of La Blanca—and Raiza.

The images and memories La Negra showed me were fuzzy and staticky like they had been recently. Pero even with the occasional hazy frame, the story of El Baca's escape was clear.

I saw El Baca huddled in the underground caverns near Ciudad Minerva. The first few months of his captivity played out in stop-motion. He'd been moved often to avoid being rescued by El Cuco's remaining cronies. Pero with El Cuco banished and El Baca captured by La Bruja and the Galipotes, it seemed as though most of the enemy had disappeared when their prison had. Pero El Baca felt and heard the tumbao, distantly, and the drums needled him every day of his imprisonment.

The images swam before my eyes as the forest shook with thunder above us. I heard the Bird baca's screeching call echo through El Bosque as the vision knit itself back together, the call seeping into the ground where El Baca was imprisoned. One baca's magic strengthened another's, allowing El Baca to break free of La Negra's chains. La Bruja had gotten there too late, but still she tried to stop him.

The picture got even hazier, like I was seeing the memory through a thick layer of smoke. I blinked and noticed that white sand was leaking through the tunnel.

"Oye, Natasha, ¿párate por favor?"

I felt Natasha's wave of La Negra churning us forward even faster.

I placed both hands against the wall and squeezed my eyes tightly, willing the memory to be clearer. Pues, it half worked, pero now they weren't moving memories, just individual images. La Bruja squared up with El Baca. La Bruja conducting a wave of black sand. And . . .

"Natasha," I whispered, pero the tunnel echoed so a hundred Pilars whispered the name.

It was unmistakably Natasha in the next slide. In the memory, my cousin's hair was braided down her back in a single plait that shone in the half-light as she ran forward, streams of La Negra surrounding each fist. Images flashed in rapid succession: El Baca rearing up and La Bruja staring on in surprise as Natasha leapt forward. La Bruja raising an arm and batting Natasha out of the way of El Baca's uppercutting claw as a long cut opened along her ribs. The next image was of La Bruja doubled over in pain and Natasha rushing to her side, El Baca disappearing into El Bosque with The Bird leering down.

And with that the memory faded, and the real Natasha stood facing me in the dim blue light of La Negra's tunnel, tears filling her wide brown eyes.

"Natasha." I reached my hand out, pero she flinched away from me.

"Don't. It was my fault. I should've been watching for the uppercut pero—"

"La Bruja wouldn't have intervened if she didn't want to—"

Natasha slammed her fist into her palm and the sand of the tunnels rippled as the echoes bounced around us. "She shouldn't have had to!" Natasha grimaced. "Did La Negra tell you how the fight above is going?"

"No," I added. "Pero I will ask."

I touched the wall tenderly and this time there were no images, pero I could hear the dim voices of people

I knew. Scratchy, but definitely the voices of Carmen and La Bruja . . . and Raiza.

"You can't fight her like this," Carmen said to La Bruja, her voice muffled in my head like she was on the other side of a long room.

"And . . . *you* . . . can't . . . fight . . . her . . . at . . . all," La Bruja's wheezed between each word. "This is bruja work."

"Tik tok MirandaaaaaaaaaHHHHHH," came a third voice, y pues only one living person would call La Bruja by her true name. Pero Raiza's words contorted at the end, like she had just broken a bone.

Had La Bruja managed to get a shot in? And what about the storm? How long until Raiza brought back a baca Jefe and turned the world upside down?

I screwed my eyes shut even tighter, straining to hear the vision of the battle above.

"What's the problem, traitor?" Carmen spat. "Baca got your tongue?"

"Insolent children!!" Raiza cursed at the top of her voice. "You have no idea the glory with which you tamper. Go bring your precious sisters, I want all to witness it."

"I'm just so—" La Bruja coughed wetly, like she was hacking up blood. "I'm so certain you never monologued this much before you bonded with that parasite."

Carmen let loose a bitter laugh.

"And I was certain, all those years in The Above," Raiza replied coldly, "that you had the decency to die in the Raid to spare me the indignity of witnessing you as this washed-up old hag."

As I strained harder to hear, the picture started to come hazily into focus, all outlines like the memory was being illustrated on a chalkboard before my very eyes. Carmen knelt with La Bruja propped against her knee, glaring at Raiza. Both of the evil bruja's hands were tethered to the storm as she sneered at the pair. Pero La Negra wasn't focused on Raiza at all, pues, she wasn't even focused on La Bruja.

The Sight came to me.

La Negra sketched five images that flickered rapidly through my mind on a loop:

1. La Bruja tapping on Carmen's leg.
2. Carmen grimacing, every line of her face a trench of twisted regret.
3. Carmen doing something I never thought I'd see: turning and running. A massive cloud of silence magic spilling from Raiza's fingertips

as Carmen sprinted. Carmen leaping into the trees, missing the cloud by inches. And leaving La Bruja behind on one knee, arms at the ready to face Raiza.

4. Four butterflies fluttering rapidly over El Bosque, each of their wings covered with La Negra's strange, intricate patterns.

The butterflies became four women, flying over El Bosque, one diving to grab Carmen and carry her toward a massive storm cloud at the edge of Zafa.

THIRTY-FOUR

WE SURFED THROUGH THE TUNNELS at warp speed and barely ground to a halt when we arrived at the destroyed cane field that had once guarded La Blanca. Natasha tore open the soil above our heads, and I shielded my eyes from a downpour of white sand. Immediately we were surrounded by the boom of thunder rattling the tunnels. Wind screamed as if the hot rain was being ripped from the bellowing clouds above. We stared up, together, into the hell Raiza was creating.

"No matter what"—I grasped Natasha's shoulder— "brujas fight as one."

Natasha nodded grimly and we leapt out of the hole to find Raiza standing over a figure.

Raiza had a ragged wild glee in her eyes, like she hadn't slept in days, as she stared down at her old rival.

She looked triumphant, power swirling around her in waves of shimmering heat. Pero it was also clear maintaining the storm on her own was taking a toll. Maybe we still had a chance to stop this. Her cheeks had sunk even further into her face, creating gaunt shadows that made her look like Svengoolie's girlfriend. Y también Raiza was swaying slowly from side to side, humming as if a strong breeze might carry her away.

But her feet stayed firmly planted as gale force winds spun small tornadoes of white sand beneath our feet. The air whipped a savage song. And there in Raiza's clutches, bleeding heavily from her mouth, was La Bruja.

Her face looked swollen and pale with blood loss. La Bruja clutched at the wound along her side with both hands as the wind threw the locks around her face like wind chimes. The rotten stench of El Bosque de las Tormentas had been replaced by the coppery smell of rain.

The storms must be aligning. The wind blew so hard it sounded like a blade and the storm clouds flashed with glimpses into a world, my world.

Trujillo's return was nearly complete.

"LET HER GO!" Natasha yelled, sending a blast of La Negra at Raiza, whose eyes flashed open as if she'd been lost in a song.

Raiza threw out her free hand without looking at Natasha and caught the blast of La Negra in a cloud of silence magic. I heard Natasha's breath catch in her lungs, pues, she was probably feeling the bone-deep nausea of watching each grain of La Negra squirm and swirl around inside the suffocating cloud, bleaching and falling to the ground, lifeless.

Raiza scowled at Natasha in disgust. "You think because you killed that foolish dog and a pigeon that I answer to you?" Raiza shook La Bruja, whose eyes rolled back in pain. "To her?"

Raiza swayed again as the wind surged past her, smelling of salt water and heat. And I could hear something, almost a song pero a dreadful, hopeless song. Like the music of bones grinding against each other, pues, a song of despair that I could almost taste.

"Let the music rise from El Mar." I heard Raiza's voice in my head.

I had to act fast, pero how could we beat Raiza? What could distract Raiza long enough to slow the spell?

I thought about how Raiza longed for power. Adoration.

Maybe we could use that against her.

I knelt, bowing my head and pressing my hand to the

ground like I was surrendering to the traitor bruja. Natasha looked at me with surprise and hurt swimming in her eyes, pero I gave her a quick "trust me" look. Natasha nodded her head the narrowest margin possible.

"You could learn something from su prima," Raiza crowed at Natasha as the wind howled around us and I heard the crack of another huge branch behind us, pues, maybe a whole tree falling in El Bosque. "She recognizes a god when she sees one."

With Raiza caught up in an ego trip, I sank my hand a little farther into the swirling sand.

Raiza conjured two shimmering clouds of silence magic around either hand. More clouds began to elongate, as if the storm were breathing life into the curse. She pointed one clouded finger at Natasha, then jabbed it at the ground.

"Kneel."

"Never." Natasha took a step forward and I heard the sound of her yanking her machete clear of its sheath.

Almost, almost, I thought to myself, wiping a bead of sweat from my brow, a knot of anxiety in my gut.

"I won't ask again." Raiza extended the cloud of silence magic around La Bruja's head. "Kneel."

La Bruja's eyes went wide, her mouth fighting for

breath. There wasn't much time left, pero I didn't need much more. I just hoped La Bruja could hang on a little while longer.

Natasha's eyes widened in fear, but her voice was steel. "You are nothing but an arrogant fool who abandoned her sisters to die. And you'll fall as you lived, alone, without anyone at your back."

Raiza barked a laugh. "I'm a goddess! I see all and I don't need anyone!"

And just then my plan exploded into motion. Pues, literally.

A geyser of black sand tore open the ground to Raiza's left, stunning the bruja traitor as she backpedaled away. The cloud of suffocating silence magic that had surrounded La Bruja vanished, and my mentor dropped to the ground like a rag doll.

"NOO!!!" Natasha and I shouted at the same time.

But we had no time to see if she was alive as Raiza dashed away from La Negra.

A goddess who sees all? Pues, it was time to put that to the test.

"NOW!!" I hollered, pero Natasha didn't need the order to take advantage. My prima was already in motion, sprinting toward Raiza, her machete a blur behind her as a crack of thunder banged against my eardrums. I plunged my other hand into the ground to direct another explosion to Raiza's right. She dodged too late and screamed as a blast of the black sand scalded the waxy, bleached skin of her elbow.

Natasha wasted no time summoning the falling grains of La Negra and pressed forward. With her uninjured arm, Raiza hurled a cloud of silence magic at Natasha, but she dodged it easily.

"A. Goddess. Stands. And. Fights. You. Coward," Natasha hollered, punctuating each word with a downward chop of her machete, forcing Raiza to retreat on her heels.

Another crack of thunder rattled all the teeth in my jaw. The clouds above writhed and meshed together, a nest of snakes summoning their master.

I sent another little stream of La Negra beneath the soil, pero Raiza backflipped away just in time and smothered the explosion with a cloud of her own silence magic. A wave of nausea roiled through me as grains of La Negra were bleached. A bolt of red lightning cracked into the ground before us, sending sand into my eyes.

Meanwhile Natasha was already at Raiza's throat, blasting the traitor across the face with a stream of La Negra that peeled away the waxy skin from the left side of her face, revealing a layer of dull bronze beneath. Raiza yelped and backhanded Natasha, who stood her ground and pushed forward.

I brushed the sand from my eyes and saw that the lightning that had struck the ground wasn't lightning at all. It was a single beam of crimson light plowing through the ground as if it was tunneling down to Hell.

Pues, or building a door to it. My eyes widened as understanding flooded my mind. *Oh no, oh no, oh no.*

Raiza's eyes glowed with triumph as she blasted another cloud at Natasha. My cousin barely had time to intend La Negra into a shield. Pero the blast was still too strong, and she stumbled back long enough for Raiza to wheel and focus her mismatched eyes on me, the waxy half of her face splitting into a grin.

"The time has come, little bruja! Soon I will rule this world and The Above, pues, even El Odio. Your order is doomed, and so are you!" Raiza pirouetted and another ring of that silence magic nearly clipped my ankle as I jumped to avoid it.

We were helpless as the wicked beam of light widened, burrowing farther into the ground while also opening an eye in the storm above us.

Raiza cackled with the remaining waxy half of her face; the other, ruined half locked in a stoic expression.

"Got any more plans?" Natasha asked as the rain of branches finally stopped.

"Make our last stand, I guess." I balled my fist and punched my open palm.

Natasha nodded and squeezed my hand and we charged toward Raiza, who was laughing with her right eye closed, the left still locked on us. I felt Natasha's strength, her fury, her fear, all pool into mine as we directed every grain of La Negra that remained with us at Raiza.

We pushed as hard as we could, the tumbao of La Negra beating a furious bachata, then a merengue, then a music too fast to identify.

Pues, maybe it was because I was so busy directing every last bit of energy I had into Intending La Negra at Raiza. Maybe it was because Natasha and I were screaming as we fought for our lives, the lives of our people. Maybe it was the thunder bellowing above our last stand as the red beam widened another yard and a thin black rectangle began to come into focus within.

Pues, maybe it was all of those things that caused us not to notice the touch of golden light that dusted the ground behind us like a new sun. Maybe that's why I didn't hear the wingbeats of the sisters as they landed behind us.

THIRTY-FIVE

A YEAR AGO, WHEN I had been matched up with El Cuco, I'd felt his entire prison tremble from the effect of what happened when you combined the power of bruja and Galipote magic. La Bruja had put aside her differences with the Galipote Sisters to create a golden wrecking ball that had smashed massive holes in the prison. I'd seen that golden light surround the five women as they conducted the comet again and again into La Blanca, causing it to collapse around me and El Cuco. Pues, sometimes in my dreams I still see it, a sun they commanded. Pero I'd never *felt* the power that flowed through La Bruja and the Galipote Sisters until Minerva placed her thin hand across my shoulder and begin to merge the sisters' power with mine and Natasha's.

It began in my feet, the music of the Galipote magic

different from the tumbao of La Negra. Not the drums, but the hum of a warm light moving through my bones. Like a choir of people singing one huge note that rose through my legs and threaded itself through my chest until every vein and pore felt as if it was bathed in sunlight.

On my left, Dede stood with one hand on my other shoulder, another blasting a stream of golden light that joined Minerva's, Maria Teresa's, and Patria's own. Their light snaked around the column of La Negra that me and Natasha were trying to sandblast through Raiza's shield.

I chanced a look at the storm's outline in the red light, and my heart dropped into my stomach as I saw that it had taken the shape of a man. Pues, no face or hands or skin had formed yet, pero I had a feeling those additions weren't far behind. I pushed myself even more as a demon Trujillo threatened to break free.

Rivers of sweat poured down my face as the Galipotes' golden lights connected and an earsplitting crack shook the trees, sending Raiza sliding backward. But she quickly recovered her footing and faced us again.

The beam of red light flickered like a bad faucet, but the outline of the man within was beginning to move. Its faceless head looked down, and it stretched the skeletal outlines of newly made fingers. As the Galipotes launched more magic the beam of red light stuttered again, and the outline of the creature within looked up at the storm as if noticing it for the first time. Its form began to become fuzzy, out of focus, like a bad dream half remembered.

"NO!" Raiza yelped desperately, and raised a trembling hand, sending another massive burst of silence magic up toward the rolling thunder.

But Dede and Minerva were ready to counter anything Raiza tried to throw at them or the storm. "I think not," they said in unison, sending a tower of golden light that exploded like a firework against the storm.

The red beam sputtered, and a mangled squawk came from within, where demon Trujillo's outline punched at the edges of the beam like it was trying to muscle its way out of the curse. Raiza stared in horror. Still, she kept her cool. For a moment.

Carmen sprung from the right and tackled Raiza, who barely had time to scream before my hermana rained down blow after blow on her waxy face.

Pues, I'd seen Carmen fight before. She was one of the best the ciguapa forces had ever seen. Pero this was another level!

The ciguapa's arms were a pair of blurs, each punch

connecting before the other arm pulled back from a blow. Even more importantly, Carmen's legs had pinned each of Raiza's arms to her sides, and the beam of red light sputtered and faded to a dull pink. The outline of the resurrecting Trujillo was still desperately pressing against the sides like a caged animal.

"What if we try to hit the beam?" Natasha's voice was trembling with exhaustion, her shirt plastered to her collarbone with sweat.

"It's worth a shot!" I Intended a bolt of La Negra that passed through the outline of the resurrected Trujillo with barely a flicker.

"Perhaps we should blast her again?" Maria Teresa asked, pointing to Raiza, who was still having her face tenderized by Carmen.

"No, we might hit Carmen!" I countered. My pulse hammered in my ears, drowning out the thunder.

"ENOUGH!!!" Raiza bellowed and a massive wave of silence magic erupted in a dome that hurled Carmen up into the sky.

Minerva and Dede put out their hands to either side of me and another blast of that golden light shattered the silence magic stampeding toward us. And then Carmen started to fall, unconscious, limbs flapping like a rag doll.

"Patria!" Minerva called to her sister, commanding steel clear in her voice.

Patria was already launching herself into the sky to scoop up Carmen. Meanwhile Raiza pushed herself to her feet, a murderous look in her eyes as she glared at the sisters, me, and Natasha. An angry purple bruise was blooming on . . . well, actually, it'd probably be easier to say where there wasn't a bruise: on the half of Raiza's face that still had the waxy, white skin of the Pariguayo. Carmen was no bruja, pero she really had a magic of her own, the magic of throwing hands.

"I'm going to go up and try to stall her," Dede said. "If we can keep her from reconnecting to the curse . . ." She beat her wings twice and took off.

"You can't play keep-away forever, Minerva!" Raiza growled, and raised both arms before shooting ten, then twenty, then thirty of the clouds of her power into the sky. Dede spun and dodged and tried to counter each, pero there were too many.

Minerva opened her mouth to holler another order, pero Maria Teresa had already taken off into the sky to provide backup.

Patria wheeled down and lay Carmen, still unconscious, behind us as she took Dede's place at my side. She gave Minerva a look that silently asked if she should go up to aid her flying sisters. Pero even with three sisters, we were fighting a losing battle. Raiza doubled down and sent an endless stream of spells like an old-school, bullet storm–style arcade game. The sister dodged and swooped, and as more and more of Raiza's magic slipped through, we all watched in horror as the beam expanded again, turning slowly from light pink to cherry red as the outline grew a face, like a gross political cartoon of Trujillo's face.

Even though Raiza was fighting alone against us, we were losing steam after battling Raiza in DR and then The Bird and El Baca, so it felt like only a matter of time until her power was too great to fend off. Pues, I wanted to move, to do *something*, pero I was too exhausted. I didn't know if I could even manage to raise my arms.

The thunder and winds roared to life again, all-consuming, and the hands of the outline were lashed with raw pink muscle and shaded in with chalky white skin. The ugly sketch of Trujillo's face grinned and laughed, pero no sound emerged.

Minerva's eyes flicked from me, to Raiza, to the growing Trujillo, now with skin up to its shoulders, trying to calculate how to win this fight. I could feel my pulse thudding, pero I couldn't move a muscle.

There I was, too exhausted to be anything but a witness to the end of the world. And then I heard a familiar voice, raspy and full of fluid say:

"Carajo, was anyone planning on stopping the feíta if I didn't show up?"

THIRTY-SIX

"OF COURSE WE WERE!" MINERVA SCOFFED.

"You're alive!!" me and Natasha exclaimed.

La Bruja snorted, and squinted her unswollen eye. She gripped the side of her robes, which were dark red with blood, pero she was standing! La Bruja cracked her knuckles against her jaw and spat blood into the sand as thunder boomed again.

"As if I'd let that . . ." She flicked a wrist dismissively at Raiza, who was still bulletstorming clouds of silence magic while two of the Galipote Sisters zoomed through the sky to try and take out as many as possible. "That thing that she's become won't have the honor of killing me. Nobody gets rid of me but me, entiendes?"

La Bruja half grinned, half grimaced at me, each of her teeth lined in red. And even though the storm clouds had begun to pound the ground with long ropes of thick red rain, I felt better. I could feel a bit of my strength returning. Pues, if La Bruja wasn't willing to die, neither were we.

"I don't know how much more power I have left," I said, flexing my arms to shake off the aches. "But we didn't kill El Baca to only come this far, entiendes?"

La Bruja cocked an eyebrow at her star pupil, a look of admiration in her eyes.

"¡¿De verdad?!" Minerva said with surprise.

"What about that maldito bird?" Patria asked.

"Pilar chopped its head off y se fue." Natasha couldn't resist a half grin as she drew a finger across her throat.

"Well then, that changes things." La Bruja grimaced in pain but gave me a similar look of admiration. "Though, I had been looking forward to killing them—"

Before La Bruja could continue, the ground exploded around us as a bolt of Raiza's silence magic sent dirt and debris flying in all directions. I rolled to avoid it, using up more of the limited energy left in my tank.

I looked up at Raiza, who grinned maniacally before taking a bolt of golden magic to the shoulder from one of the sisters. Her smile faltered for just a second, and she scowled as if she'd just been burned.

I turned to La Bruja, who shook dirt from her thick braids. "Yo, is it just me or is Raiza weakening?"

"Good eye." La Bruja half grinned. "Well, it may not look like it, but dearest Raiza's connection to El Odio is weak now. Oye, Patria, can you still fly?"

"Yes." Patria nodded, straightening her spine.

"All right, would you please fly up there with Minerva and try to shoot down as many of those silencios as you can?"

"What about you all?" Minerva asked, eyes full of concern. "We're not leaving you behind."

"That's right." La Bruja winced and clutched her side. "You're not *leaving* us behind. Pero if I know Raiza, she won't be able to resist showing off her powers even when she's running on fumes, entiendes?"

Minerva nodded to Patria and rose into the sky to join her sisters in blocking as many of Raiza's attacks as they could, each mariposa diving and blasting like fighter planes.

La Bruja looked at me and Natasha, eyes shining with pride. "Pilar, am I correct in assuming you have a plan?"

I nodded.

I doubted Raiza could hear me over all the noise, but just in case, I used La Negra to Intend the details to La Bruja and Natasha. Natasha nodded solemnly.

But La Bruja's eyes lit up. "I like it. When you want to cut down a tree, you start at the root, not the branches. And I won't be denied my revenge. Not by Trujillo, and certainly not by Raiza."

We had to act fast. Even as Raiza's knees quivered from the strain of thrusting burst after burst of her evil power into the sky, the beam of red light intensified, and Trujillo almost looked like a person. The beige military uniform had begun to shade in around El Jefe's feet. Pero the face was still grotesque and cartoonish, not a human face at all.

"¿Brujas, listas?" La Bruja barked, sinking into a fighting stance as me and Natasha both nodded in response and positioned ourselves near La Negra's tunnels.

Wordlessly, we all Intended streams of La Negra, our strength pouring into one another in one unbreakable braid of Intention at the already occupied Raiza. She was still hurling curses at the Galipote Sisters and occasionally sidestepping a burst of golden light sent by Minerva. But clearly her reaction time was getting slower, porque she barely had time to throw out a hand to shield herself from the incoming wave of our collected bruja power.

"¡No pares!" I bellowed, the tumbao churning through each of us at a tempo I didn't even know was possible.

I dug deep and looked across the stream of La Negra to see Natasha, teeth gritted, eyebrows knit together with pure concentration. I grunted and focused even harder on Intending La Negra past Raiza's defense. Pues, either this would kill me, or Trujillo would, pero in the immortal words of La Bruja, nobody gets rid of me but me. Pues, nobody was going to erase *us* but *us*.

My thoughts were interrupted by a yowl of pain. I shot a look over at La Bruja, pero it hadn't been her; it had been Raiza. La Negra was forcing her way through, past Raiza's defenses. Steam rose from her waxy skin as she fought for release from the grains of La Negra marching up her arm.

"Almost there!" Natasha shouted as I saw the beam of red light flicker with Trujillo still trapped inside, his face the only part of him that still wasn't flesh and bone.

Raiza was still screaming as the flood of La Negra continued along her arm, burning the Pariguayo's power out of her like a parasite. She stopped firing into the sky and directed her power at the grains of black sand. I felt that wave of nausea again, but I gritted my teeth.

"Hang on tight!" La Bruja called as the red beam flickered to light pink and the grotesque lines of Trujillo's face contorted in silent rage.

I looked him in the eyes as I dug deep one last time, searching for every ounce of power I had left. Focusing on how each grain of La Negra was a part of us, our memory, our music, our gente. This man who had taken everything from Mami, from Abuela, from Natasha, was a threat to all of it.

"This time, stay dead," I said coldly, and Intended one last huge burst of La Negra from the tunnel.

It came in a tidal wave of pitch-black sand and washed over Raiza before she could defend herself. A mushroom cloud of steam burst from beneath the mound of La Negra that Raiza was buried beneath. I felt the last of my strength leave me as I collapsed to my knees and put a hand out to stop myself from falling face-forward. Natasha was at my side in seconds, arms trembling as she tried to pull me to my feet. I looked up at her, long black hair wreathed in sunlight.

Wait, sunlight?

I blinked and looked around to see the cursed weather giving way to relentless golden sunlight. The scab of brick-colored storm clouds wavered and died. I looked at the Trujillo whose face stretched demonically in a wordless scream as the beam of red light collapsed, taking him with it. It left a circle of gray ash, like an extinguished cigar.

THIRTY-SEVEN

LA NEGRA HAD SPAT ROSA'S and the Pariguayo's unconscious bodies out onto the battleground. Rosa was almost more skeletal than Raiza, with light, oak-colored skin and high cheekbones. She looked like she hadn't eaten anything in years. Pero the Pariguayo was way worse off. The separation had left Trujillo's once right hand a husk of himself. No, literally—dude looked like the outside of a white cockroach. Super gross.

"Oye, he's like an old, crunchy snakeskin y nada mas." Natasha's lip curled in disgust.

The Pariguayo let out a low hiss of fury and shuddered as he tried to get up, pero all the strength had left his body. I leaned forward, staring at his cracked teeth. He puckered his lips, his voice thin like a pile of crisp leaves. "You will all, someday—" The Pariguayo's mouth drooped into a frown of concentration as he tried to force the words out. "I . . . will . . . find a way." He coughed, and even without features, I knew he was glaring at all of us.

Including La Bruja, who staggered up behind me to the feet of her rival and the demon she'd fused herself to so many years ago. Y pues, I've seen La Bruja look El Cuco right in the eye and call him a furball. Pero this time it was La Bruja's turn to be silent as a white-hot fury hardened behind her eyes and she took a deep breath, bringing her palms together. Without a word, she brought her weathered brown hands together as a blade of La Negra cleaved the husk of El Pariguayo in two.

Pero Raiza, or Rosa again now, was a different story, spluttering up grains of La Negra. La Bruja limped over to her and crouched down with Natasha's help as the Galipote Sisters landed behind her. Rosa's pale eyes went wide with fury. She held her hand out y todo to send a shot of silence magic at La Bruja, pero nothing happened.

She tried again. Nada.

La Bruja scowled at her old friend.

"I think we severed her connection with El Odio

forever." Natasha put a hand on my shoulder. "And, of course, La Negra doesn't trust her now either."

"She still knows too much to be left alive." La Bruja stared unblinkingly at Rosa, whose dirty white dress billowed around her starved form. "If she did this once—"

"There must be a trial," said Minerva.

La Bruja turned to face the sisters and jerked her head in the direction of the Pariguayo's lifeless shell. "I already made my choice. I wasn't asking for permission."

Minerva wrinkled her nose at the husk. "What's done is done, but—"

"What part of 'I won't be denied my revenge' was unclear?" La Bruja waved off Natasha, pushing herself up.

"None of it," Dede answered. "Pero there's a difference between killing that . . . thing, and this."

Rosa's wide, pale eyes burned with hatred as she hacked up more grains of La Negra.

"We must be better than her," Minerva added. "We cannot stoop to her level of evil."

La Bruja looked back down at Rosa and grimaced in disgust, but then something softened behind her eyes. Maybe seeing her back in her original form, though a shell of the friend she'd been to La Bruja centuries ago, had changed the old bruja's mind. "Fine, there will be a trial. It's more than she ever offered any of our sisters. It's more than Cielo got."

"Don't you dare say that name!" Rosa's voice was harsh, as if she hadn't said a word in decades. "You know—"

"Oh, so you do speak." La Bruja waved off the words. "Take her away, before I change my mind."

"Rosa Perez, also known as Raiza, you stand accused of treason," began Minerva, her illustrious wings fluttering behind her. "How do you plead before this tribunal?"

Next to me, La Bruja snorted and rolled her eyes. "Pues, accused? She was taunting us only a day and a half ago with how much more mighty she was than the entire Bruja Nation. Wasn't that her plea?"

Maria Teresa side-eyed her.

La Bruja did make a solid point though. The official feel of Rosa's trial didn't make a ton of sense since everyone who was on the tribunal, including me, had been undoing Raiza's plot less than a week ago. Look, I'm not saying that we should have skipped straight to the sentencing, pero part of me just didn't see why we needed to be formally introducing someone who had tried to kill me two or three times in twenty-four hours . . .

Still, the sisters demanded it, so Carmen, Natasha, La Bruja, and I sat next to them on the raised platform at the end of the Hall of the Galipotes. Rosa stood before us, her wrists linked together by cuffs made of La Negra.

She glared defiantly at each of us. "Guilty."

"What a surprise." La Bruja's voice dripped with sarcasm as she leaned her chair back.

"Miranda, please." Patria pinched the bridge of her nose.

"Please, what?" La Bruja put her chair back on all fours. "She just told you she was guilty of treason. She sold my sisters out, she left all of us to die, and we're here playing courtroom."

"Would you have us simply kill her, like El Cuco would have?" Dede responded, a hint of steel in her voice.

"Yes, Miranda," Rosa crooned in a spookily accurate impression of La Bruja's sarcastic voice. "Tell them all about your big, brave plan to kill a defenseless woman."

La Bruja began to rise from her seat, pero Natasha snatched her soft hand. La Bruja shook her gray-tipped locks from her face and sat back down with a furious expression. "This is why I didn't want to come today . . ."

"Then why are you here?" Rosa stared daggers at La Bruja.

"Because I want to hear you say why," La Bruja spat back. "I want you to explain it to *me, maldita*. I waited hundreds of years for this moment."

And with that, she folded her arms. Silence rang in the orange half-light. Pues, maybe it was just having battled Raiza, pero I hated awkward silences even more than I used to.

"So explain it to her," I said, surprised by the power in my voice.

"What do you care?" Rosa snarled. "You weren't here, you weren't born. You come around for a couple of days and"—Rosa snapped her fingers, rattling the cuffs in my direction—"now your face is on the door of an island I gave everything to protect."

I felt every muscle in La Bruja's body tense next to me and turned my head to see her eyes wide with quiet rage.

"I watched my people die," Rosa continued. "We were going to lose the war, that was already decided, porque everyone here cared more about 'community' and the 'Bruja code' and the mighty 'La Negra' than they cared about being as strong as we could be on our own. They chose their precious rules over *survival*."

I tried not to bite at the obvious bait, pero it was difficult.

Luckily La Bruja was . . . let's just say, not as worried about that. "Oh yes, because when I don't want to lose a fight, I form an alliance with the person trying to kill me, my friends, and my family. Brujas whose children you held, who fed you, even Trainer Nina"—I noticed Rosa flinch at the mention of the trainer—"all of them went to bed one night and *never* woke up." La Bruja slammed her fist into her hand. "*You* did that. You turned your back on us because of your arrogance."

"I turned my back porque I'm a survivor. Pues, was it the noble thing you wanted from me, Miranda? You know I asked you to come with me. Did you want me to stay and die with you?"

Before anyone could react, La Bruja was up and out of her seat in a blur, and her pocketknife was pressed to Rosa's throat.

Rosa didn't flinch. Pues, if she hadn't tried to assassinate me earlier, I'd have been impressed.

"La Bruja, don't!" Minerva's voice was all steel.

"Do you people think this is a game!?" La Bruja

shouted, knife deadly still in her hand as the rest of her shook with fury.

She wheeled back to Rosa.

"You make all the jokes you want. I hope wherever you go after I kill you, everyone we loved, the last remnants of the culture you destroyed, are waiting for you."

THIRTY-EIGHT

"WAIT!!" I FOUND MYSELF STANDING before I could stop myself.

"This doesn't concern you, Pilar." La Bruja didn't turn around, eyes still locked on her once rival.

"Yes it does!" I stamped my foot, the echo ricocheting around the hall as all eyes turned to me.

"Do you know where I got this knife, Pilar?" La Bruja said, still not turning around.

"It was Rosa's. She used to throw it in the air when she was bored on stakeouts."

"How did you know that?" Rosa hissed at me, then looked at La Bruja. "How did you find that?"

Rosa's eyes went wide, and for the first time she looked the way she had before she'd fused with the

Pariguayo. Behind her eyes, part of her was always going to be that girl.

And that's what I was counting on.

"La Negra showed me a vision of your fight with the Pariguayo," I answered. "I know you fought bravely. You used to believe in something besides yourself."

Rosa flinched a tiny amount, and I walked forward slowly.

"You believed in the Bruja nation. You keep saying you don't need anyone, pero you had a funny way of showing it."

"You don't know anything about me." Rosa's voice strained, pero she didn't move porque the knife was still at her throat. "You think because La Negra showed you that little parlor trick you know what's in my heart?"

"No." I spread my hands, continuing to march forward. "I don't know what's in your heart, pero I've seen what was. You're alone porque you made it that way. You tried to summon Trujillo, you paired up with El Baca, you fused with your mortal enemy. Pues, you miss being a bruja."

"Liar!!" She hissed, pero I continued.

"You want to die spitting in everyone's face? Fine." I placed my hand on La Bruja's arm, the thin muscles tensing beneath. "Pero don't die because you think what you've done can't be healed."

"It can't." Now it was La Bruja's turn to growl. "It can't be undone. You should know that as well as anyone, Pilar. Don't insult my sisters by—"

"She didn't say undone," Natasha piped up, scurrying to my side. "She said *healed.*"

And then, more quietly, Natasha whispered to me, "If you have a point to make, you should probably get there soon."

I nodded and turned to face La Bruja. "You said Rosa was a prodigy, right?"

"It hardly matters now." La Bruja rolled her eyes.

"Please, I need you to trust me. You said she was a prodigy, yes?"

"Yes," La Bruja said curtly, lowering the knife for a moment to point at me then at Rosa, "which is why I say she's too dangerous to leave alive."

I reached out my hand, but La Bruja flinched away from it.

"Maybe the same thing that makes her dangerous is also what makes her useful?" I asked, slowly tasting the words. "She nearly destroyed the Bruja nation once, and now it's just the three of us. Pero there will be more of us. And now that she's lost her powers, maybe she can help you teach a new generation of brujas the culture."

La Bruja's eyes went wide, her brows furrowed, and for a moment I wondered if she was going to hit me.

"What's more important?" I said quickly. "Rebuilding the Bruja culture with everything she knows about the balance between La Negra and El Odio, or getting revenge?"

La Bruja paused, eyes narrowing and shifting out of focus like she was trying to solve a math problem. She was at least thinking about it—that was something, right?

La Bruja lowered the knife and hurled it to the ground, inches from Rosa's feet. The ding of metal against stone filled the hall, and Rosa recoiled at the sound.

"I will never forgive you for what you've done," La Bruja said slowly and coldly to Rosa. "Thanks to you, there are too few brujas left on Zafa for me to kill you without hurting the nation. I will not forgive you. If it were up to me, you'd be as dead as . . ." La Bruja's lip trembled, and then she steeled her jaw.

"But," she continued, "the brujita makes a point. I thought the nation was lost forever until she came along. It may never be what it was because of you, and even if it is someday I will never forgive what you've done. But for now, for the nation, I'll give you a chance to make it as right as you can."

And with that, La Bruja swept out the doors, and was gone.

THIRTY-NINE

"YOU'RE SURE YOU WANT TO do this?" I asked Natasha.

"Yes, Prima!" Natasha answered back, a wry smile twitching at the corner of her mouth the way Abuela's does sometimes. "Just like the previous hundred times you asked."

"I'm just saying that it's gonna be, like, a lot, entiendes?"

"Y'know, for a girl who saved the island twice you have some weird opinions about what's going to be intense."

"I'm just saying that—" I felt Natasha's warm hand on my shoulder.

"Pilar, every day I was in La Blanca I only thought about two things: escape and Grecia."

I smiled as the light passed through the broad leaves of palm trees, whispering to itself in the slight breeze.

Once, Natasha and Mami had lived a block apart, then worlds apart, but they stayed connected as one like sisters. And even after Natasha had disappeared, they grieved as one.

"I'm ready for this. Plus, I know the . . . como se dice . . . 'special effects' in your *documentary* sound pretty realistic, but it's still probably best if you show up with the star of the show, just to be safe!"

"Why are you like this?" I groaned, giving Natasha a side-eye.

"Have you met you?" Natasha quipped. "It's in our blood, Prima!"

A couple moments later we were back at a familiar scene. Within a secluded grove of trees stood Carmen, the Galipotes, and even Gray Locks. I chanced a side-long look at Natasha. Her shoulders slumped a bit, pero she straightened back up almost immediately.

"I'm sorry, Prima, I really thought she'd come."

Nobody had seen or heard from La Bruja since Rosa's sentencing.

"Y'all know we'll be back to visit, like, all the time now that we won't have to keep this world a secret from my family, right?" I said, pulling Carmen into a fierce hug.

Carmen held me at arm's length. "Hermanita, if living through the war taught me anything, it's to make sure you make every goodbye with your family count."

"The ones who share your blood"—Carmen nodded at Natasha—"and the ones you chose."

Carmen pulled me into her mane of black curls, and I felt her heartbeat, just a half second behind my own.

"Plus, Zafa owes you, both of you, an unpayable debt," Minerva said, presenting each of us with one of the black roses from the balconies of Ciudad Minerva.

Carmen gave a loud cough that sounded suspiciously close to "I was there too." But Minerva either didn't hear her or decided to ignore it.

"You gave us back our lives, our cities y también you gave us permission to hope."

"I still don't really understand what *exactly* a doc-u-mentry is?" Carmen looked to me for confirmation that she'd said the word correctly; I took pity and just nodded. "Pero I've never seen you be anything but brave, brilliant, and super annoying to anyone who stands in the way of you doing what you want to do, so . . ."

Natasha snorted with laughter—why was I bringing her back with me again?

"I guess what I'm saying is, no matter where you walk, hermana, your path is already illuminated," Carmen finished.

"Agreed," said Gray Locks. "You make the impossible look routine. And I finally got to retire because of you. But I had to come see you off."

"Don't you still teach four days a week?" Carmen cocked an eyebrow.

"Have to stay active. I'm retired, not dead, Carmen." Gray Locks glowered at Carmen, who rolled her eyes.

"Indeed," said a voice waiting above in the trees. "Otherwise she'll get even softer. The Yaydil I know would have checked this tree at least three times and stationed a guard before going anywhere near it."

La Bruja jokingly clicked her tongue as all of us stared up at her. She chucked the rest of the apple she'd been cutting and front flipped down from her branch.

"I thought you weren't going to come," me and Natasha said at the same time.

La Bruja frowned a little, then nodded. "I needed some time on my own . . . to think."

"But you were on your own for hundreds of years . . ." Yaydil jabbed.

"Yes, and every minute I spend in conversations like this makes me miss it even more." La Bruja spat an apple seed onto the ground.

"Natasha, I've only had one daughter in my lifetime." La Bruja squeezed Carmen's shoulder. "One daughter, until you. I thought I'd lost everything I could lose, pero you are helping me build it again. I love you, mija."

La Bruja's chin began to tremble, so she hugged Natasha for support. Natasha closed her eyes and buried her face in La Bruja's sleeve as the two stood there slowly swaying to a music only they could hear.

La Bruja turned and squared her shoulders to me like a prizefighter. Then she pulled me in for a rib-cracking hug and spoke quietly in my ear. "You came here by accident, pero thank you. I lived so many years never thinking I would get to see the day the Bruja nation could make plans to rebuild. I thought I was the last bruja. Thank you for helping mine become one story among thousands again."

I didn't know what to say so I just hugged her even tighter, drinking in her scent of pine and coconut, which would soon be a memory until next time our paths crossed—hopefully not with some huge crisis. Like maybe in February I could just steal down from Chicago to Zafa and enjoy some time on the beach, watching the snow-white waves roll in instead of being in the actual . . . well, snow.

"Okay, listo, Natasha?" I asked, pulling the Olvida from my back pocket.

Natasha spread her fingers, closed her eyes, and drank in the smells of Zafa again. Then she nodded, and we took each other's hands as we stepped onto the page.

I opened my eyes, and we were greeted by the miniature honks of small delivery vans and the mosquito drone of dirt bikes cutting through the streets of Santo Domingo.

When we arrived at the apartment I climbed the stairs and knocked on the front door. Before I could even knock a second time the door flew open, and there was Lorena.

"OH MY GOD! PILAR, WHERE HAVE YOU BEEN?!" Lorena's words spilled out of her mouth at record speed.

"Well, actually, it's a bit of a funny story—!" I

started, but Lorena punched me in the shoulder. "OW!"

"We've been worried sick about you! The storm of the century comes and goes, and you disappear in a country where you barely speak the language."

"Hey, I get by—" I tried to interject, but Lorena was building up steam, the kind that made her a champion debater.

It was starting to give me a headache.

"And another thing: Mami has been *losing* it. Losing it! I think you disappearing must have triggered some kind of trauma response porque she's saying that she saw you with . . ." Lorena's jaw fell slack as she finally noticed the identically sized brown girl standing next to me.

Y pues, there was probably a classier way to handle this, pero I'd lived in the same house with Lorena for ten years and I think I'd seen her speechless like three times. So I let her marinate in it for a little while.

Finally, I cleared my throat. "Like I said, it's kind of a funny story."

"Hi, Prima!" Natasha waved weakly from behind me.

FORTY

I'VE SEEN A THOUSAND SHOTS I wish I'd caught in my strange, beautiful, death-defying, magical thirteen years. The tiny moon of a Fisher-Price baseball that Lorena batted into the sky and over the top of the old lightbulb factory around the block from us, the ocean zooming below us as we landed in DR, Carmen punching a Cucito so hard it took out the three that were standing behind it like fuzzy, smelly, vicious bowling pins. Pero the moment Mami fell to her knees on the tiled floor and pulled me deep into her arms, the moment when she held me at arm's length roughly, as if she were about to launch into a hall of fame parent lecture about responsibility and worry y todo, the moment when she looked over my shoulder and saw Natasha—that look, pues, I'm glad it's just hers.

Mami stood slowly, and Natasha stepped forward tentatively, as if they were two girls on the opposite sides of a dream they knew had to end.

Pues, I thought, *how many nights in La Blanca did they dream of this?*

Mami looked at Natasha as Abuela sat slack-jawed on the couch.

Natasha cleared her throat, opened her mouth and made a little choked noise, then shut it again. She tried a second time and got out a couple words. "Grecia, I—" Pero Mami bounded toward her and swept my lost cousin into a tremendous hug with a grito that could have peeled the paint off walls.

"No, no, no," Mami wept, tears sprinting down her cheeks and then disappearing in Natasha's pitch-black hair. "No, I won't believe it. No, no, no."

She swayed back and forth, still weeping silently as Abuela looked at Lorena, whose eyes were darting back and forth between me and Natasha. Already Mami's string of noes was drifting from insistent to almost a lullaby as she rocked back and forth. Natasha was shaking with tears, her whole body vibrating with the love of two primas closer than sisters.

Lorena finally found her voice. "Umm, so, hermanita. I think I speak for all of us when I say—"

"Negrita," Abuela cut in, "where in the hell have you been?"

I blinked three times at Abuela. I'd made a nearly feature-length movie about this whole wild adventure, pero something told me that I was going to have to lead with my words on this one.

"Okay, well, don't be mad." I took a deep breath as I saw Abuela's eyebrows rise in warning. "All right, all right, that ship sailed, gotchu!" I tucked a curl behind my ear, took a deep breath, and began. "Last summer, when I went to Dominguez's office—"

"LAST SUMMER?!?!" responded everyone but Natasha, who wiped a tear from her puffy eyes and gave me a just-like-we-rehearsed nod.

I scratched the back of my head. "Let me begin again. After all, I'm paid to believe in what I can see."

Everyone sat slack-jawed as I finished the *very* broad strokes version of my story—how I'd rescued Natasha, defeated El Cuco, and recently defeated Raiza and stopped Trujillo coming back. All free of charge, by the way—de nada, world, next one's going to cost you.

"So," Lorena began again for the hundredth time, "you have, like, magic powers?"

"Yes."

"And this whole storm—that was . . . you?"

I closed my eyes so nobody could see me roll them. "No, that was Raiza."

"Who is now Rosa?" Abuela added, confused.

"I mean, sorta?" I shrugged at Natasha, who was huddled next to Mami on the couch.

"And that's how we got lured here . . . ," Lorena said, "by this maldita? She made a fake foundation and gave Dominguez money?"

I nodded patiently. As patiently as I could, at least.

"I'll kill her myself," Mami said flatly.

"Pero, Mami, I—"

"Nobody tries to kill my daughter and just . . . walks away. I'm going to track her down, and then we'll see who's a bruja, entiendes? I'll go right down to La Plaza, hop in that hole, and strangle that payasa."

"Grecia." Natasha tugged lightly at Mami's sleeve. "I just got you back after decades—centuries in my time—can your death wish wait a few weeks at least?"

"Yeah, Mami, you don't—" Suddenly Mami's words sank in. "Wait, the curse was broken! What hole?"

FORTY-ONE

GOTTA SAY, "OPENED A PERMANENT portal between Santo Domingo and a remote corner of a magical forest" has to be the greatest "What I did over summer vacation" of all time! That the portal exists because someone was trying to kill me . . . I mean, who needs to get caught up in the details?

The important thing is that as the sun rose over La Plaza, I could hear the storm of El Bosque de las Tormentas in the rustling of the trees below. The glowing ring of white light and the swaying branches of the trees below were all that made it clear that this wasn't just a regular manhole in front of the building that had once been Trujillo's palace.

"See, hermanita, told you it was really there!"

Lorena chimed as we nudged our way closer to the front of a huge crowd of onlookers.

Classic Lorena—tell her there's another world, our cousin's still alive, and magic is real, and she'll still find an "I told you so" in there somewhere. Pues, maybe that's *her* magic.

I shrugged, looked back at the portal, and felt a massive grin spread across my face. Why should we be the only family to get their long-lost people back? Pues, maybe now Zafa and our world could be friends, partners, entiendes?

I wanted to spend more time thinking of all the hugs and tears decades in the making that were about to happen, everything the world was about to learn. I looked at Mami holding Natasha by the shoulders, her same beautiful, dark bronze hands that used to cradle Natasha's only picture now dabbing tears of joy from her eyes.

"Negrita," Mami said warmly to me. "No hay palabras, ni en ingles, ni en español. I couldn't be prouder of you, either of you."

I smiled broadly and looked at Natasha.

"Y también," Mami said, still smiling, "if you ever do something this dangerous again, I will take away all your editing software for a *year*."

Cold dread filled my stomach. That was more terrifying than facing El Cuco; he was just a demon, but Mami's my *mom*, entiendes?

Mami swallowed hard and smiled sadly. She turned to Natasha. "I just can't believe we've got you back forever now."

"Well, part of the year," Natasha said, voice muffled into Mami's shoulder.

"Wait, what?" Lorena asked.

"Natasha's going to be um . . . como se dice? Commuting?" I said, wincing.

"It's just that, like I told Pilar the last time I saw her, I don't belong to this world anymore. Well, not all the way," Natasha said as we walked the cobblestones of Calle de las Damas. "And La Bruja is going to need a lot of help rebuilding the nation. So I'll be here in the summer and spring."

"And in Zafa during the winter and fall, teaching and training new brujas," I finished. "Porque somebody is too good for the Chicago winter."

"Too good for it? Pilar, I don't know if I'd survive it! And I went to La Blanca!" Natasha huffed, barely stifling a nervous grin.

Mami spoke up. "In that case, we'll have to make plans for tomorrow."

263

"Grecia, I'm not going back to Zafa tomorrow?" Natasha cocked her head to the side in confusion.

"Yes, but we are leaving DR tomorrow. And after fifty Natasha-less years, you know what I could use? A trip to the dang beach."

EPILOGUE

"EVERY DAY I WAS IN that awful place, I would imagine us at Boca Chica, not a care in the world." Natasha smiled, though a little sadly.

Abuela sat in the front seat of our rental car humming softly to herself, the brown slopes of her shoulders baking in the crisp gold of the midday sun. Today was going to be our last day in DR.

A different song swayed out of each passing car as me and Natasha looked around. A husky tío-looking dude with gold caps patted the hood of our car gently, pointing over at a congested parking lot.

"¿Cuanto?" Abuela asked, without rolling down the window.

The gold-toothed tío smiled proudly. "Dos mil pesos!"

265

"Payaso!" Abuela exclaimed. "Keep driving, Grecia. We'll have to find another parking lot!"

"Oye, Doña," the gold-toothed tío said, throwing his hand exaggeratedly over his heart like he was acting out his death onstage. "I meant no offense!"

Abuela and the tío continued to haggle, and eventually their voices faded into a rapid back and forth. Abuela finally won the debate, and the tío agreed to take two hundred pesos and not a penny more. Abuela grinned in satisfaction and patted Natasha's leg without looking back, eyes as always on the horizon.

Past the little shack restaurant that smelled of mouthwatering fried fish, I looked at my cousin, standing on the beach, palms open wide. The Mariposa de dos Mundos was finally back beneath her own sun.

As I stared at Natasha, grinning ear to ear, I felt Mami's warm brown hand on my shoulder.

"Do you know what your papi said to me when we brought you home from the hospital?"

Mami had never mentioned this story, and I was shocked that with all of the times I'd interviewed her I'd never thought to ask. If Mira Paredez could see this . . . ugh.

"He said that he could tell already that Lorena

was going to be one of the smartest daughters anyone could ever have."

Typical; even when we were talking about me, we were still talking about Lorena.

"And I asked him," Mami continued, "well, what do you think Pilar will be? And your papi laughed that laugh of his and clapped his hands together. And he said, 'Grecia, I couldn't guess, pero she's your daughter, so I'd bet anything she's going to do something impossible.'"

I gulped as tears pricked my eyes. I threw my arms around Mami as Natasha sprinted toward the water. The sand in her hair winked like stars as she jogged into the water. Pues, she was just a kid at the beach for the first time in who knew how long.

"You two coming?" Lorena asked, flashing that thousand-watt smile as she ran to join Natasha in the water.

"Tranquilase," Abuela said at my shoulder. "It's not like the ocean is going anywhere."

I laughed as I took her and Mami's hands on either side of me and we walked calmly toward where Lorena was straining not to keep peppering Natasha with questions about how magic worked, and the Trujillato, and everything we'd been through. And when I stepped into the water, pues, for a moment I forgot all of that. I closed my eyes, just smelling the fried fish and hearing the jingle of beach vendors hauling around novelty shot glasses, T-shirts, even aguacate!

I opened my eyes and saw why Natasha would come back to a memory of here when it felt like all other lights had gone out. The water lapped against our ankles as the wind dusted the tops of the trees, turning them into chismosas. I took Natasha's hand in mine, and we all stood in a row: Abuela, Lorena, Mami, Natasha, and me, the breeze making us squint toward the horizon as a golden light shone on each of us. This was one of the most beautiful places in the world, and only a deep evil could have made it anything else.

Pero we'd passed under the shadow of two worlds worth of evil and destruction, and now each of us was a link in a chain, a whole lineage of women who did more than survive: We built tomorrow ourselves. Together, we would make this place home again.